La Chamade

By Françoise Sagan

La Chamade

Françoise Sagan

Translated from the French
by Robert Westhoff

E. P. Dutton & Co., Inc.
New York
1966

English translation copyright, ©, 1966 by E. P. Dutton & Co., Inc., New York, and John Murray Ltd., London / All rights reserved. Printed in the U.S.A. / No part of this book may be reproduced in any form without permission in writing from the publisher, except by a reviewer who wishes to quote brief passages in connection with a review written for inclusion in a magazine, newspaper or broadcast. / Published simultaneously in Canada by Clarke, Irwin & Company Limited, Toronto and Vancouver / Library of Congress Catalog Card Number: 66-21294 / Published in France 1965 by René Julliard under the title *La Chamade* / Copyright, ©, 1965 by René Julliard, Paris

FIRST EDITION

Grateful acknowledgment is made for permission to quote from *The Wild Palms* by William Faulkner © copyright, 1939, by Random House, Inc.

To my parents

I have made the magical study
Of Happiness, that no man eludes.

RIMBAUD

Part One

Spring

1

She opened her eyes. A bluff, determined wind had entered the room, billowing the curtain into a sail, bending the flowers in a large vase on the floor, and now attacked her sleep. It was a spring wind, the first: it smelled of earth, woods, forests; and having swept unscathed over the suburbs of Paris and the streets reeking of gasoline fumes, it arrived, brisk and swaggering, in her room, at dawn, to point out, even before she was awake, the pleasure of living.

She shut her eyes, rolled over on her stomach, and groped for the clock on the floor, her head still buried in the pillow. She must have forgotten it; she always forgot everything. Rising cautiously, she opened the window and looked out. It was dark, and the windows facing hers were closed. That wind had no sense or it would not be about so early. She went back to bed, energetically arranged the blankets around her, and for a while pretended to sleep.

In vain. The wind paraded about the room; she sensed that it was vexed by the lush, nodding roses, the frightened swell of the curtains. It passed over her at times, pleading with all its country scents: "Come for a stroll, come for a stroll with me." Her sluggish body refused the invitation, snatches of dreams clouded her brain, but her lips slowly relaxed into a smile. Dawn, the country at dawn . . . the four plane trees on the terrace, their leaves sharply outlined against a white sky, the crunch of gravel under a dog's paws, eternal childhood. What could still give some charm to childhood after the lamentations of writers, the theories of psychoanalysts, and the hasty effusions of all humans when the subject was broached: "When I was a child . . ."?

Doubtless only a nostalgia for a supreme, lost sense of irresponsibility. But (she never would have wanted to tell anyone) she had not lost it. She felt thoroughly irresponsible.

This last idea got her out of bed. She glanced about the room for her dressing gown without finding it. Someone must have put it away, but where? She opened the wardrobe with a sigh; she would never become accustomed to this room. Nor to any other, for that matter. She was wholly indifferent to her surroundings. Yet hers was a lovely, high-ceilinged room, with a grayish-blue carpet and two large windows opening onto a Left Bank street. The bed resembled an island flanked by two lonely reefs: a bedside stand and a low table between the windows, exceptionally good antiques, according to Charles. And the dressing gown, finally discovered, was silk, and luxury, in fact, something most agreeable.

She walked into Charles's room. He slept with closed windows, his bedside lamp lighted, and no wind had ever disturbed him. His sleeping pills lay neatly by a pack of cigarettes, a lighter, an alarm clock set for eight o'clock, and a bottle of mineral water. The only untidy thing in the room was an evening paper on the floor. She sat at the foot of the bed, staring at him. Charles was a man of fifty with good, softish features and an unhappy look when he slept. He seemed even sadder than usual that morning. He had real-estate affairs, was wealthy, and his relations with others were rather difficult because of a mixture of shyness and courtesy that sometimes resulted in coldness. They had been living together for two years, if the fact of occupying the same flat, seeing the same people and sometimes sharing the same bed could be called living together. He moaned slightly and turned toward the wall. She thought, once again, that he must be unhappy because of her, and immediately reflected that, however you looked at it, he would have been unhappy with any woman twenty years his junior with an independent spirit. She picked up a cigarette from the bedside table, lighted it noiselessly, and resumed her contemplation. Charles's hair was graying on top, his mouth losing color, and the veins stood out on his beautiful hands. A wave of tenderness swept over her. How could one be so good, so intelligent, and so unhappy? She could do nothing for him: no one could console a man for being born and then having to die. She began to cough; it was a mistake to smoke in the morning on an empty stomach. One mustn't smoke on an empty stomach or drink alcohol or drive fast or make love too much or overtax one's heart or spend money, or anything else. She yawned. The thing to do was to take the car and follow the spring wind far into the country. And she would not work that day, no more that day than she did on any other. She had, thanks to Charles, lost the habit.

Half an hour later she was speeding along the highway to Nancy. The convertible's radio was broadcasting a concerto. Was it Grieg? Schumann? Rachmaninoff? Surely a romantic composer, but which one? The uncertainty annoyed, yet pleased her. Her only care for culture was through memory, a perceptive memory. "I've heard it dozens of times; I know that I was unhappy then and that the music seemed to be transferred to that suffering like a decal." She had already forgotten who had made her suffer; perhaps she was already growing old. But that was of little importance. It had been a long time since she had thought about herself, looked at herself, defined herself in her own eyes, and now only the present drove with her in the dawn wind.

2

The noise made by the car in the courtyard woke Charles. He heard Lucile singing to herself as she closed the garage doors, and wondered with amazement what time it could be. His watch showed eight o'clock. He thought for a moment that Lucile must be ill, but the sound of her gay voice below reassured him. He was tempted to open the window, to stop her, but refrained. This exhilaration he knew so well in her; the exhilaration of solitude. He shut his eyes for an instant: that was the first of the thousand impulses he must check that day so as not to bother Lucile, so as not to encumber Lucile. Had he been fifteen years younger, he would perhaps have opened the window and called out in a commanding but casual voice, "Lucile, come on up; I'm awake." And she would have run upstairs to drink a cup of tea with him. She would have sat on his bed, and he would have sent her into gales of laughter with his witty remarks. He shrugged his shoulders. Even fifteen years ago he could not have made her laugh. He had never been amusing. To be nonchalant was something he had discovered only a year ago, thanks to her. Nonchalance . . . one of the longest and most difficult studies, apparently, unless you had a natural aptitude for it.

He sat up and looked with astonishment at the ashtray near him. There was a stubbed-out cigarette, and he wondered if he could have forgotten to empty it the night before. That was impossible. Lucile must have come in and smoked. In fact, a small hollow in the bed showed where she had sat. He was a quiet sleeper and a very tidy one; the maids who had watched over his bachelor life had often enough praised him for it. It was one of the things for which he had always been congratulated: his calm, sleeping or awake; his self-possession; his good education. Some people were praised for their charm, but that never happened to him, at least not in an entirely honest way. What a pity. He would have felt as though someone had robed him in glistening plumage, soft and marvelous. Certain words made him suffer cruelly, calmly, like a faded souvenir: "charm, ease, unconcern" and, Heaven only knows why, "balcony."

He had once mentioned this to Lucile; not about the first words, of course, but the last. "Balcony"? She had repeated, "balcony, balcony," then asked if he ever thought of the word in the plural. He had said yes. She inquired whether balconies had played any part in his childhood, and he had replied no. Lucile had stared at him, intrigued, and, as happened each time she looked at him with an expression that was not merely kind, a wild hope had stirred him. But she had mumbled something from Baudelaire about balconies in the sky, and their talk had gone no further. No further, as usual. And yet he loved her; he could not let her know how much he loved her. Not that she would have taken advantage of it, but the fact would have troubled, saddened her. That she had not left him was already beyond his hopes. Security was the only thing he could offer her, and that, he knew, was the least of her worries. Perhaps.

He rang. Then, gathering up the newspaper from the floor, he made an effort to read. It was hopeless. Lucile must be driving too fast, as usual, in the convertible he had given her for Christmas. He had asked one of his friends at *Auto-Journal* to find out which was the best sports car, the most secure, the steadiest, but had told Lucile that it had been the easiest car to get, pretending to have ordered it by chance the day before and, as he expressed it, "on the spur of the moment." She had been delighted. But suppose they telephoned to say that a dark blue convertible had been found overturned on a highway, a young woman pinned under it whose papers . . . He got up. All this was idiotic.

Pauline came in with the breakfast tray. He smiled.

"What's the weather like?"

"Grayish, but there's a smell of spring in the air."

She was sixty and had been in his service for the past ten years. Lyric expressions were not her custom.

"Spring?" he repeated absently.

"Yes, that's what Miss Lucile told me. She was in the kitchen before I came down, took an orange and said she must be off, that there was a smell of spring in the air."

She smiled. At first Charles had been afraid that she might resent Lucile, but after two impatient months, Pauline's moral attitude had taken shape: "Lucile is ten years old mentally, and you, sir, aren't a bit older, so you can't be expected to protect her efficiently against the twists and turns of life. That will have to be my duty." And with admirable energy, she ordered Lucile to rest, to eat, to avoid drinking; and Lucile, apparently delighted, obeyed. It was one of the minor mysteries in his household that Charles thought curious but at the same time charming.

"She only took an orange?" he asked.

"Yes. And she said to tell you to breathe deeply when you went out because there was a smell of spring in the air."

Pauline's voice was expressionless. Did she realize that he had begged her for a message from Lucile? She sometimes averted her eyes when he spoke to her, and he felt that what she blamed was not Lucile but the form of his passion for her. A starved, sorrowful passion that Pauline alone was allowed to suspect, one that seemed inexplicable to the sensible woman who had accepted Lucile's personality in a maternal and slightly condescending way. She might have complained, perhaps, had he fallen in love with what she called a "wicked woman" instead of a "nice girl." She did not know that the latter could be worse than the former.

3

Claire Santré's flat had been sumptuous in poor Santré's time. It was less so at present, as could be seen in the sparse furnishings, the blue curtains dyed a dozen times over, and the hired butler's haggard expression as he wondered, for just a moment too long, which of the five drawing-room doors led to the pantry. Nevertheless, it was one of the most agreeable apartments on the Avenue Montaigne, and Claire's invitations were much sought after. She was tall, spare, and energetic, the sort of blonde who might well have been a brunette. She was a little over fifty, did not look her age, and talked gaily of love, like a woman who was no longer an interested party but who had kept pleasant memories. Consequently, women liked her, and men flirted with her in a boisterous, impudent manner. She was a part of the small brave regiment of middle-aged women who somehow manage, in Paris, to live and to remain fashionable and sometimes even to set the fashion. Claire always invited one or two Americans and one or two Venezuelans to her big dinners, explaining that she was obliged to, even if they were not amusing, because she did business with them. They would be seated next to some society queen, straining to follow a conversation composed of enigmas, obscure allusions, and incomprehensible jokes. It could only be hoped that all this would be joyously repeated back in Caracas. In return, Claire's hospitality was rewarded with exclusive rights to Venezuelan fabrics, and her parties never lacked whisky. Above all, she was a clever woman and never spoke ill of anyone, unless it was absolutely necessary in order not to appear stupid.

Charles Blassans-Lignières had been, for ten years, one of the pillars of Claire's dinners. He had lent her a great deal of money, and never spoke of it to her. He was rich, he was handsome, he spoke little but well, and from time to time, resignedly chose a mistress from among Claire's protégées. The affair would last a year, sometimes two. He took them to Italy in August and sent them to Saint-Tropez when they complained of the summer heat, or in winter to Megève, if they grumbled about feeling tired. The liaison ended with a handsome present, ended usually without any apparent reason and, six months later, Claire would "take him in hand" once more. But for the last two years the quiet, businesslike Charles had escaped her attentions. He was head over heels in love with Lucile, and Lucile was a most elusive person. She was gay, polite, often amusing, but stubbornly refused to talk about herself or Charles or their plans for the future. Before meeting Charles, she had worked for a small paper, the kind that pretended to be Leftist in order to pay its employees badly—and whose bold opinions went no further. She rarely worked there now, and the truth was that no one had the faintest idea of how she spent her time. If she had another lover, he did not belong to Claire's set, although Claire had sent scouts reconnoitering without success. Her imagination exhausted, Claire had suggested to Lucile a little Balzacian intrigue of the sort commonly practiced in Paris which would have provided Lucile with a mink coat, plus a check from Charles amounting to the price of the mink coat.

"I don't need money," Lucile had said. "And I detest that sort of business."

She spoke dryly, without looking at Claire, who after a moment of panic had one of the strokes of genius that justified her career. She took Lucile's hands in hers.

"Thank you, my dear. You must understand, I love Charles like a brother and I know you so slightly. Excuse me. Had you accepted, I should have been afraid for him, that's all."

Lucile had burst into laughter, and Claire, who had vaguely hoped for a moving little scene, remained anxious until, at a dinner, she saw Charles again exactly as he had always been. Lucile knew how to hold her tongue. Or perhaps, to forget.

In any case, that spring appeared to be marked for disaster. Claire muttered to herself as she examined the table arrangements. Johnny, the first guest to arrive, according to a time-honored agreement, followed her like a shadow. He had been a homosexual until the age of forty-five, but now, after a day's work and a dinner, felt incapable of meeting a handsome young man at midnight. He was content to follow them with melancholy eyes in the drawing rooms. Worldly society kills everything, even vice. Pious souls must give it that much credit. So Johnny had become Claire's devoted escort. He accompanied her to dress rehearsals, to dinners and helped at her receptions, self-consciously but with admirable tact. His name was Jean, but as everybody thought that Johnny sounded gayer, he bowed to the inevitable and, in the course of twenty years, had even acquired a faintly British accent.

"Whom are you thinking about, my pet? You seem so nervous."

"I was thinking about Charles. I was thinking about Diane. As you know, she's bringing love's young dream along with her. I've only seen him once, but I'm not counting on him to enliven the dinner. How can one be thirty, so good looking and so gloomy?"

"Diane's great mistake is falling for intellectuals. It's never been a success for her."

"Some intellectuals are amusing," said Claire with indulgence, "but Antoine is not an intellectual: he confines himself to editing a series of books at Renoard's. And how much does an editor make? Nothing. You know that as well as I do. Diane's fortune, thank Heaven, is sufficient for—"

"I don't believe he cares much about money," said Johnny feebly, for he thought Antoine very handsome.

"Oh, he'll come to it," said Claire in the weary voice of experience. "Diane is forty and has millions; he's thirty and earns two hundred thousand francs a month. That sort of equation can't last."

Johnny began to laugh but stopped suddenly. He had used an antiwrinkle cream recommended by Pierre-André and had not had time to let it dry thoroughly. He would have to remain stone-faced until eight thirty. As it happened, it was eight thirty already. He laughed again, and Claire threw him an astonished glance. Johnny was an angel, but the bullet or two he got when playing the hero serving with the R.A.F. in 1942 must have done something to his brain. A . . . what was it, a lobe? yes, a lobe must have been affected. She looked at him with amusement. To think that those long white hands, now too delicately arranging the flowers on the table, had grasped a machine gun, a joystick, and brought in flaming planes in the middle of night. . . . Human beings were so often surprising. One never knew "everything" about them. Actually, that was the reason why she was never bored. She gave a long, satisfied sigh, cut short by the stiff belting around her waist. Cardin went too far when he pictured her as a sylph.

Lucile tried to disguise a yawn, done by breathing in through the corners of her mouth, then exhaling softly between the front teeth. It resulted in a rather rabbit-like appearance, but one's eyes did not fill with tears afterward. The dinner seemed interminable. She sat between Johnny, who had been anxiously patting his face since the meal began, and a quiet, handsome young man, said to be Diane Merbel's new lover. The silence, however, did not bother her. She hadn't the least desire to fascinate anyone that evening. She had been up too early. She tried to remember the odor of that devilish spring wind, and closed her eyes for a moment. She was surprised, on opening them, to find that Diane was staring harshly at her. Was Diane so much in love with the young man, or jealous? She looked at him: he had ash-blond hair and a firm, determined chin. He kneaded a bit of bread into a ball. There was a whole row of them round his plate. The conversation turned to the theater. An excellent topic, for Claire adored a play that Diane loathed. Lucile made an effort and turned toward the young man.

"Have you seen the play?"

"No. I never go to the theater. And you?"

"Very rarely. Last time, I saw that charming English comedy at the Atelier, with an actress who was later killed in an automobile accident. What was her name? I've forgotten."

"Sarah," he said softly, and laid both hands flat on the tablecloth.

His expression petrified Lucile for a second. She thought suddenly: My God, he's really unhappy!

"Forgive me," she said.

He turned toward her and asked, "What?" in a dreary voice. He no longer saw her. She could hear him breathing, unevenly, like a man who had received a shock, and the idea that she had caused it, although unintentionally, hurt her deeply. She took no pleasure in being insolent, and even less in being cruel.

"What are you dreaming about, Antoine?"

Diane's voice had a strange sound, just a shade too light, and created a silence. Antoine did not answer: he seemed blind and deaf.

"He really is dreaming, and no mistake," said Claire, laughing. "Antoine, Antoine . . ."

Nothing. Now there was a dead silence. Forks in hand, motionless, the guests watched the pale young man as he sat staring at a not very interesting decanter in the center of the table. Lucile quickly laid her hand on his sleeve, and he stirred:

"What did you say?"

"I said you were dreaming," replied Diane curtly, "and we wondered what about. Is it indiscreet?"

"It's always indiscreet," interposed Charles.

He looked attentively at Antoine now, like everyone else. Antoine had arrived as Diane's latest lover, possibly her gigolo, and now suddenly he had become a young dreamer. A gust of envy, of nostalgia, passed over the table.

And, in Claire's mind, a gust of spite. After all, this was a dinner for the happy few, the well known, brilliant, amusing, in touch with everything. The young man should have listened, approved, laughed. If he was dreaming of a dinner with some schoolgirl in a Latin Quarter snack bar, he had only to leave Diane, one of the most charming and fashionable women in Paris. And one who wore her forty-five years better than most. Except tonight; she was pale and watchful. If she had not known her so well, Claire might have thought Diane was unhappy. She continued:

24

"I bet you were dreaming about a Ferrari. Carlos bought the latest model. He took me for a ride in it the other day, and I thought my last hour had come. And Heaven knows he's a good driver!" she added with a share of surprise, for Carlos was heir to some throne or other and she thought it exceptional that he should be able to do anything but sit in the Crillon lobby, waiting for the return of the monarchy.

Antoine turned to Lucile, and smiled. He had light-brown, almost yellow eyes, a straight nose, a wide, handsome mouth, and a certain virility that contrasted with the fairness of his hair.

"Please forgive me," he said in a low voice. "You must think me very rude."

He looked at her squarely; his eyes did not wander idly over her shoulders or the tablecloth, as men's usually do, and he seemed to exclude completely the rest of the table.

"We've exchanged three sentences and begged each other's pardon twice," said Lucile.

"We're beginning at the end," he answered gaily. "Couples always end by asking pardon, or at least one of the two does. 'I beg your pardon but I don't love you any-more.'"

"That's still quite elegant. Personally, what irks me is the honest approach: 'I beg your pardon; I thought I loved you; I was mistaken. It's my duty to tell you so.'"

"That can't have happened to you often," said Antoine.

"Thank you very much!"

"I mean that you can't have given many men the chance to say it. Your bags would have been packed and waiting in a taxi."

"Particularly since my luggage consists of two sweaters and a toothbrush," said Lucile with a laugh.

He paused, then: "Oh? I thought you were Blassans-Lignières' mistress."

What a pity, she thought quickly. I thought he was intelligent. For her there was no possibility of coexistence between gratuitous malice and intelligence.

"That's true," she replied, "you're quite right. If I left now, it would be in my car, with lots of dresses. Charles is very generous."

She had spoken calmly. Antoine lowered his eyes.

"Forgive me. I detest this dinner and this group."

"Then don't come here any more. At your age, it's dangerous anyway."

"You know, little one," said Antoine, suddenly irritated, "I'm most certainly older than you."

She broke into laughter. Diane and Charles regarded them fixedly. They had been placed next to each other at the other end of the table, facing their "protégés": the parents on one side, the children on the other. Children of thirty who refused to play at being grown-up. Lucile stopped laughing: she did nothing with her life, loved no one. If she were not so happy to be alive, she would have killed herself.

Antoine laughed. Diane suffered. She had seen him laugh with another. He never laughed with her. She would have even preferred that he kiss Lucile. It was frightening, that laugh, his suddenly youthful expression. What were they laughing about? Diane glanced at Charles, but he was watching them fondly. Charles had become idiotic in the last two years. Lucile had charm and very good manners, but she was neither a beauty nor an intellectual phenomenon. Nor was Antoine, for that matter. She had had other men better looking than Antoine, and mad about her. Yes, mad. But it was Antoine that she loved. She loved him; she wanted him to love her, and someday she would have him at her mercy. He would forget that dear departed actress, and she, Diane, would be everything to him. Sarah . . .

how often she had heard that name: Sarah. He had spoken of her at first, until one day, exasperated, she had told him that Sarah had been unfaithful to him, that everyone knew. He had said blankly, "I knew it too." And they had never mentioned her name again. But he whispered it in his sleep. Soon . . . soon, when he turned over in his sleep and stretched his arm over her body in the dark, it would be her own name he would whisper. Suddenly, she felt her eyes fill with tears. She began to cough, and Charles patted her gently on the back. This dinner seemed endless. Claire Santré had drunk a little too much, as happened to her more and more frequently. She discussed paintings with an assurance that far surpassed her knowledge, and Johnny, a connoisseur, was visibly suffering.

"Well," said Claire in conclusion, "when this young fellow showed up with that thing under his arm, when I turned it to the light, thinking my sight was failing me, do you know what I said?"

The guests wearily shook their heads.

"I said: 'Monsieur, I thought I had eyes to see with, but I was mistaken; I see nothing on your canvas, Monsieur, absolutely nothing.' "

And with an eloquent gesture, no doubt intended to illustrate the picture's emptiness, she upset her wineglass on the tablecloth. Everybody seized the opportunity to get up, Lucile and Antoine with heads lowered to hide their uncontrollable laughter.

4

There can never be enough said of the virtues, the dangers, the powers of a shared laugh. Love can no more do without it than can friendship, desire, or despair. Between Antoine and Lucile, it was the impromptu laugh of students. The two of them, desired, pampered, loved by serious adults, knowing they would be punished in one way or another, gave in to their helpless laughter in a corner of the drawing room. Parisian etiquette, even if it separates lovers during dinner, nonetheless calls for a short truce afterward, when one recovers his bedmate for an exchange of gossip, loving words, or reprovals. Diane waited for Antoine to rejoin her, and Charles had already taken the first step in Lucile's direction. But the latter obstinately continued to look out the window, her eyes filled with tears, and the moment her glance fell upon Antoine standing nearby, she quickly turned away while he hid his face behind a handkerchief. Claire tried to ignore them, but it was evident that an atmosphere of jealousy and rancor now dominated the drawing room. She sent Johnny on his way with a nod of her head that signified "Tell those children to behave themselves or they won't be invited again," a nod of the head that, unfortunately, was seen by Antoine, who, overcome anew, was forced to prop himself against the wall. Johnny assumed a gay expression:

"For Heaven's sake, tell me what it's all about, Lucile; I'm dying of curiosity."

"Nothing," said Lucile, "nothing, absolutely nothing; that's what makes it so terrible."

"Terrible," echoed Antoine. He was completely disheveled, youthful, wonderful, and Johnny felt a moment of violent desire.

But Diane arrived. She was angry, and anger was becoming to her. Her superb bearing, her celebrated green eyes, her extreme slenderness made her a spirited war-horse.

"What can you have found to say to each other that is so funny?" she asked in a voice tinged with doubt and indulgence, but especially doubt.

"Us? Oh, nothing," said Antoine innocently. And the "us" that she had never obtained from him for any project, for any memory, brought Diane's fury to a climax.

"Then stop conducting yourselves in such a vulgar manner. If you aren't amusing, at least be polite."

There was a short silence. Lucile thought it normal that Diane scolded her lover, but the use of the plural seemed slightly excessive to her.

"You're losing your head," she said. "It's not your business to forbid me to laugh."

"Nor me," said Antoine slowly.

"Excuse me, I'm tired," said Diane. "Good night. Could you escort me?" she asked poor Charles, who had approached them.

Charles assented, and Lucile smiled at him:

"I'll join you at home."

Their departure caused the sort of hubbub that follows a flare-up, everyone speaking of something else for several minutes before concentrating on the details, and Lucile and Antoine remained alone. She leaned on the balcony and looked at him pensively. He calmly smoked.

"I'm sorry," she said. "I should have controlled my temper."

"Come," he replied, "I'll take you home before it becomes dramatic."

Claire, with an understanding expression, saw them to

the door. They were quite right in leaving, but she remembered so well what it was to be young. They formed a charming couple. She could help them . . . but no, there was Charles; where was her mind tonight?

Paris was black, glowing, seductive, and they decided to walk home.

The relief they first felt on seeing the door shut on Claire's look of false conspiracy changed suddenly into a desire to leave, to know, in any case to finish with a sort of violence, this disjointed evening.

Lucile had no intention, not even for a second, of playing the role so tacitly insinuated in the expressions of the others when she had said good-bye: that of the young woman who deserts her aging protector for a handsome young man. She had told Charles one day, "I shall make you unhappy, perhaps, but never ridiculous." And, in fact, the few times that she had been unfaithful to him he could have suspected nothing.

This evening was absurd. What was she doing in the street with this stranger? She turned to him, and smiled.

"Don't look so gloomy," he said. "We'll stop for a drink on the way."

But they had several. They stopped at five bars, avoiding two because it was obviously unbearable for Antoine to enter with someone other than Sarah, and they talked. They crossed and recrossed the Seine as they talked, walked up the Rue de Rivoli as far as the Concorde, entered Harry's Bar, and left again. The morning wind had begun. Lucile reeled from sleepiness, whisky, and his attention.

"She was unfaithful to me," said Antoine. "The poor thing thought that to sleep with producers or journalists was the thing to do. She lied to me continually, and I despised her as I played the proud, the ironic, the judge. By what right, dear God? She loved me, yes, she must have loved me, because she had nothing to gain. . . .

"That night, the eve of her death, she almost begged me to stop her from leaving for Deauville. But I told her: 'Go ahead, go if it amuses you.' What an ass, what a conceited ass I was!"

They crossed a bridge. He questioned her.

"I've never understood anything about anything," said Lucile. "Life seemed logical enough until I left my parents. I wanted to take a degree in Paris. I dreamed. Since then, I've looked for parents everywhere, in my lovers, in my friends. I'm content to have nothing of my own, not the smallest plan, not the tiniest worry. I'm in tune with life. It's strange; I don't know why, something in me harmonizes with life the moment I awaken. I shall never change. What can I do? Work? I'm not talented. I must fall in love, perhaps, like you. Antoine, Antoine, what are you doing with Diane?"

"She loves me," said Antoine. "And I like tall, slim women. Sarah was short and fat, and it moved me to tears. Can you understand that? And what's more, she bored me."

Fatigue became him. They walked slowly up the Rue du Bac and entered a brightly lit café. They gazed at each other frankly, without a smile, without a frown. The juke-box played an old Strauss waltz, and a drunk attempted, lurchingly, to dance at the other end of the bar. It's late, it's so late, whined a small voice inside Lucile. Charles must be mad with anxiety. Go home; you aren't even interested in this boy.

And suddenly she felt her cheek against Antoine's coat. He held her against him with one arm, his head touching her hair, and he said nothing. She felt a strange tranquillity steal over them. The proprietor, the drunk, the music, the lights had always existed; or, perhaps, she had never existed herself. She didn't understand anything any more. They took a taxi to her door and they said good-bye politely, without another word.

5

But they were soon to see each other again. Diane had made a scene, and after that not a woman present at the dinner would have imagined inviting Diane without Charles, or more exactly, Antoine without Lucile. Diane had changed camps: she had left the tyrant's camp, where she had played such an able part for twenty years, to join the victims. She was jealous; she had shown it; she was lost. Quiet rumors of the kill floated on the spring air. By one of the curious turnabouts so typical of her set, the things that had contributed to her force and her prestige had now become liabilities: her beauty "not like when she was young," her jewels "not enough" (when the least among them would have been more than enough for any one of her friends the week before), down to her Rolls-Royce: "at least she has that." Poor Diane: envy had turned itself inside-out like a glove; she would wear out her face with cosmetics, bruise her heart against her diamonds, go riding with her Pekingese in the Rolls. At last, at last she could be pitied.

She was aware of all that. She knew Paris well and had had the good fortune, at thirty, to have married an intelligent writer who had pointed out the workings of the machinery before fleeing, horrified himself. Diane had a certain courage that was due to her Irish ancestry, a sadistic nurse who had brought her up, and a private fortune that

32

permitted her to do as she pleased without bowing to anyone. Say what you like, adversity humbles the spirit, especially a woman's. And Diane, who had more or less escaped
all passion, had never paid more attention to a man than
he did to her, now saw herself, with horror, spying on
Antoine. And already she was thinking of other means
than passion to bind him to her.

What did he want? He wasn't interested in money. His
publisher paid him a ridiculous salary, and he flatly refused
to take her out when he couldn't afford it. That meant that
they often had dinner, the two of them, at her flat, an idea
that would have been unthinkable only six months earlier.
Fortunately there were the first nights, suppers and dinners, the festivities offered gratuitously to the rich in Paris.
Antoine sometimes said vaguely that books were his only
interest and that one day he would succeed in the publishing business. And, in fact, at the dinners he came alive only
if he found someone willing to discuss literature with him
rather seriously. As literary lovers were in style that year,
Diane, stimulated slightly, had spoken to him of the Prix
Goncourt, but he had insisted that he didn't know how to
write and, more important, that knowing how was indispensable in producing a book. She had been persistent just
the same: "I'm sure that if you really wanted . . . Think
of that young X . . ." "Oh, no, no!" had cried Antoine,
who never raised his voice. No, he would finish his life as
a reader at Renoard's, with two hundred thousand francs
a month, and would still be mourning Sarah fifty years
later. Meanwhile, Diane loved him.

She had spent a sleepless night after Claire's dinner: Antoine had returned at dawn, probably drunk, and gone
straight to his room. She had telephoned him every hour,
ready to hang up at the sound of his voice. She wanted only

to know where he was. At six thirty he had answered at last, murmuring simply, "I'm sleepy," without even asking who it was. He must have made the round of bars at Saint-Germain, perhaps with Lucile. She wouldn't speak to him of Lucile; one must never put a name to one's fear.

The next day she telephoned Claire to apologize for having left so abruptly: she had had such a terrible headache all evening.

"I noticed that you didn't look very well," said Claire, always understanding and affable.

"I'm not getting any younger," replied Diane coldly. "And young men are so exhausting."

Claire laughed knowingly. She adored allusions, or more exactly, intimate details, and no one could be more precise in describing the technical qualities of a lover than two women of the world talking together. It was as if the constant use of passionate adjectives for their dressmakers had left only the dry terms of weights and measures for their lovers. Claire grew restless; Diane's conversation was leading nowhere. She made the first move:

"Our little Lucile is a bit irritating with her schoolgirl giggling. She's nearing thirty, isn't she?"

"She has pretty gray eyes," said Diane, "and if it amuses Charles . . ."

"Nevertheless, two years with her must seem long," sighed Claire.

"With him, too, my dear; don't forget that." And with this kindly remark they laughed and hung up. Diane thought that she had arranged the incident. And Claire could say that dear, flighty Diane had phoned at noon to excuse herself. She had forgotten a fundamental principle of Parisians, that one must never apologize and that anything is permitted provided that it is done gaily.

So Johnny, at Claire's request, had an invitation sent to

34

Charles Blassans-Lignières for a first-night performance to which Diane had also been asked. It was agreed that they would have supper somewhere afterward, "only friends." Apart from the amusement to be had from the meeting of Antoine and Lucile, Claire had the assurance that Charles would automatically pick up the check. Very convenient: Johnny was near ruin at the moment, Diane could not be allowed to settle the bill, and Claire didn't remember if she had thought to invite an extra wealthy man. The species had become precious and extremely rare at a time when only homosexuals were kept on a really grand scale. Anyway, the play was certain to be amusing because it was by Bijou Dubois and Bijou Dubois knew what made good theater.

"You can say what you like, my pet," she remarked to Johnny in the taxi that drove them to the Atelier, "I've had enough of your modern theater. To see the actors sitting in armchairs on stage, to listen to their flat recitations of the facts of life bores me to death. I prefer vaudeville. Johnny, are you listening?"

Johnny, to whom she was making this speech for the tenth time this season, nodded his head. Claire was charming, but her vitality exhausted him, and he had a sudden urge to get out of the car and walk up the Boulevard de Clichy, which was swarming with people, to eat French-fried potatoes out of a paper sack, to be beaten by a tough. Claire's intrigues seemed too simple, and he was always surprised to see them succeed.

The theater guests were milling about the Place Dancourt exchanging greetings and banal remarks, assuring one another that this was the prettiest theater in Paris and that the little square was too provincial for words. Lucile came out of a café, escorted by Charles, sat down on a park bench and began to eat an enormous sandwich. After a moment's hesitation, several others followed suit. Diane's car drove up noiselessly and, by chance, came to a stop just in front of the bench. Antoine stepped out, helped Diane, and turned, to see Lucile with her mouth full, happy, as Charles, embarrassed, rise to greet Diane.

"You're picnicking? What a good idea," said Diane.

She had seen out of the corner of her eye that on other benches Edmée de Guilt, Doudou Wilson, and Madame Bert were doing the same thing.

"It's nine; the play won't begin for another fifteen minutes. Antoine, be an angel and run get me a sandwich. I'm famished," she continued.

Antoine hesitated. Lucile saw him look at the café, then at Diane, and finally, with a vague gesture of resignation, he crossed the street and pushed open the door of the café. She could see the proprietor get quickly to his feet, come from behind the counter and, with a pained expression, shake Antoine's hand. The waiter did the same. All she could see of Antoine was his back, but she had the impression that he was retreating, floundering under a hail of blows. Then she remembered: Sarah. The same theater, the rehearsals, the café where Antoine must have waited. Where he had never returned.

"But what can Antoine be doing?" asked Diane. "Has he taken to solitary drinking?"

"Sarah," said Lucile without looking at her.

The name bothered her, but she couldn't have questioned Antoine or even mentioned it. He came toward them, expressionless, like a blind man. Diane understood suddenly, and turned toward her so brusquely that Lucile recoiled, startled. And, in fact, Diane had almost slapped her.

So Lucile knew about Sarah, too. She had no right to know. Antoine belonged to her, Antoine's laughter and

Antoine's sorrow. It was on her shoulder that he dreamed of Sarah each night. It was Diane that he preferred to the memory of Sarah. The bell rang for the first act. She took Antoine's arm, leading him. He followed, dazed. He politely greeted several critics, some friends of Diane's, and helped her to her seat. The curtain went up, and in the dark she leaned toward him.

"You poor darling," she said . . .

And she took his hand in hers.

6

During the intermission, they split into two groups. Lucile and Antoine smiled at each other from a distance and, for the first time, with feeling. He watched her as she talked, absently leaning against Charles's shoulder, and the curve of her neck, the faintly amused line of her mouth attracted him. He wanted to push his way through the crowd and take her in his arms. It had been a long time since he had felt desire, simple desire for an unknown woman. She turned at that precise moment, met Antoine's eyes and, sensing the meaning in them, stood motionless before offering a small embarrassed smile. She had never really thought of Antoine physically; it took this look of desire to make her appreciate his beauty. All her life it had been like that; by some happy chance or an almost pathological dislike of difficulties, she only took an interest in those who were interested in her. And now, her back turned to him, she saw Antoine's handsome mouth again, the golden color of his eyes, and she asked herself by what extraordinary coincidence they had not kissed that first night. Charles felt her head move from his shoulder, glanced at her, and immediately recognized the thoughtful, gentle, almost re-signed expression she always had when she took a liking to a man. He turned and saw Antoine.

After the play, they again formed into a group. Claire was in ecstasy over the performance, the lovely weather, the maharani's jewels; she was delirious with pleasure. They couldn't agree on a restaurant, as usual. Finally they decided to go to Marnes, for obviously the green grass and fresh air were just what Claire needed. Diane's chauffeur stood waiting.

"Diane," said Charles suddenly, "would you take me with you? We came here in Lucile's convertible, and I'm feeling old tonight and I have a cold. Can you do without Antoine?"

Diane did not turn a hair, but Claire rolled her eyes in amazement and disbelief.

"Why, of course," said Diane. "See you later, Antoine, and don't drive too fast."

The four of them got into the Rolls-Royce. Lucile and Antoine were left on the sidewalk, slightly stunned. Neither Charles nor Diane looked back, but Claire's part-ing wink froze them though they pretended not to have seen it. Lucile was lost in thought. It was very much like Charles to inflict suffering on himself, but how had he sus-pected a desire of which she had become conscious only an hour before? She had never been unfaithful to Charles except with someone she was certain he would never meet. If there was anything in the world that she loathed, it was the complicity of two lovers behind the back of a third, and the intrigued laughter of witnesses like Claire. None of that for her! Antoine laid his hand on her shoulder, and she shook her head. After all, life was simple enough, the weather fine, and she liked the young man. We'll see soon enough, she thought. During thirty years on earth the number of times she had thought "We'll see soon enough" was staggering. She began to laugh.

"Why are you laughing?" asked Antoine.

"I'm laughing at myself. The car is a few steps away. What have I done with the keys? Will you drive?"

Antoine drove. They rode without speaking at first, breathing the night air in the open car, ill at ease. Antoine drove slowly. They had reached the Etoile when he turned to her.

"What made Charles do that?" he asked.

"I don't know."

They realized at once that with these two sentences they admitted and ratified the furtive glance they had exchanged during the intermission, that something existed between them that could no longer be removed. She should have replied, "Do what?" and transformed Charles's suggestion into the prudent decision of a man with a cold. Too late. Her only desire was to reach the restaurant quickly. Or that Antoine would make some coarse gesture, some vulgar remark, so she could be finished with him. But Antoine said nothing. They drove through the Bois de Boulogne now; they followed the Seine; they must have looked like specimens of gilded youth, two sweethearts in a purring sports car: she, the daughter of Dupont Steel, he, the son of Dubois Sugar, they would marry next week in the cathedral, with the families' consent. They would have two children.

"Here's another bridge," remarked Antoine, heading for Marnes. "The number of bridges we've crossed together."

This was the first allusion to the other evening. Lucile suddenly remembered how she had hidden her face in his coat in the little café. She had completely forgotten.

"So we have; yes, it's true. . . ."

She made a vague movement of her hand, and Antoine

took it in mid-air, squeezed it gently, kept it in his. They drove into the Parc de Saint-Cloud. Now come, thought Lucile, he's holding my hand while we cross the park; it's spring, no cause for alarm; I'm no longer sixteen. But her heart thumped; she felt the blood drain from her face and hands, rush to her throat, choke her. When he stopped the car, she felt dazed. He took her in his arms, kissed her furiously, and she noticed that he trembled as much as she did. He sat back; he looked at her and she looked back at him, completely motionless, until he leaned toward her again. He kissed her slowly now, gravely. He kissed her temples, her cheeks, returned to her mouth; and seeing his face, calm, attentive, over hers, she knew that she would often see it like that. There was nothing she could do to resist him. She had forgotten that one could want another so much. She must have dreamed of it. How long ago? Two years, three years? But she couldn't recall another face.

Antoine buried his face in Lucile's hair. "What's come over me?" he said anxiously. "What's come over me?"

She smiled; he could feel the movement of her cheek against his, and he smiled too.

"We must drive on," she whispered.

"No," said Antoine. After an instant he moved away from her, and in the anguish they so quickly felt, they understood.

Antoine started off hurriedly, and Lucile haphazardly touched up her face. The Rolls was already there, and they realized that their car might have passed it in Paris, and it could have arrived behind them in the park, surprising them with its headlights, like two night birds. But it was there, reigning over the little square, the symbol of power, of luxury, of their bonds, and the little sports car next to it seemed absurdly young and frail.

40

Lucile removed her makeup. She was totally exhausted, and contemplated the tiny wrinkles that showed at her mouth and eyelids, wondered what they meant, who or what had caused them. They were not the lines of passion, of effort. They were probably the marks of facility, idleness, distraction, and for a moment she loathed herself. She ran her hand over her brow. She had felt disgust for herself frequently during the last year. She must see a doctor. A question of blood pressure, no doubt. She would take a few vitamins and she could gaily continue throwing, or dreaming, her life away. She heard herself call out rather angrily:

"Charles! Why did you leave me alone with Antoine?"

At the same time, she knew that what she really wanted was a scene, a scandal, anything but this quiet disgust. And it was Charles who would pay, Charles who would suffer. That she only liked extremes was one thing, that she made others put up with them was something else. But the question had already left, like a javelin, crossing her bedroom, the landing, to hit Charles as he undressed slowly in his own room. He was so tired that, for a second, he thought of dodging the query and replying, "Really, Lucile, I had a cold." She would not have been insistent: her search for truth never went very far. But he was too anxious to know, to suffer; he had lost forever the taste for security that had made it so easy for him to close his eyes to his mistresses' infidelities for the past twenty years. He answered:

"I thought you had a fancy for him."

Instead of turning, he looked at himself in the mirror, and was surprised his face had not grown pale.

"Have you decided to throw me into the arms of all the men I fancy?"

"Don't be annoyed with me, Lucile. In this case it's too bad a sign."

41

But she had already crossed the room; she slipped her arms around his neck, murmuring "pardons" indistinctly. All he could see was the reflection of Lucile's dark hair on his shoulder, a long strand on his arm, and he felt the same heartache, the same sorrow. "She's all that I love; she'll never really belong to me. She will leave me." And at that moment how could he possibly imagine loving another lock of hair, another human being? Love's strength probably lies in a sense of the irreparable.

"That's not what I meant," said Lucile, "but I wouldn't like . . ."

"You wouldn't like me to be accommodating," said Charles, turning to her. "Rest assured, I'm not. I just wanted to make sure of something, that's all."

"What did you find?"

"Your expression as you entered the restaurant, your way of not looking at him. I know you. You're attracted to him."

Lucile broke away from him.

"And so?" she asked. "Is it really impossible to find a man attractive without making someone else suffer? Will I never be at peace? What are these laws? What have you done with liberty? With, with . . ."

She was confused, she stammered, and she had the impression of having been—always—misunderstood.

"I've done nothing with my liberty," said Charles with a smile, "and you know that I'm in love with you. And it seems to me that you still have yours. As things stand, Antoine pleases you. It will turn into something or it won't; maybe I'll know and maybe not. There's nothing I can do."

He lay on the bed in his dressing gown, and Lucile stood facing him. He sat up on the edge of the bed.

"It's true," she said dreamily. "I think him attractive."
They looked at each other.

"And if anything happens, will you be hurt?" asked Lucile.

"Yes," said Charles. "Why?"

"Because otherwise I'd leave you," she said, half stretched on Charles's bed, head in hand, knees doubled up to her chin, her expression relaxed. Two minutes later, she was asleep, and Charles Blassans-Lignières had trouble in giving each of them a fair share of the blankets.

7

He got her telephone number from Johnny and called her the next morning. They met at four o'clock in the semi-student, semi-junior-executive room where he lived, on the Rue de Poitiers. She took no notice of the room at first; all she saw was Antoine, who kissed her without a word, without a greeting, as if they had not been parted for a second since the park at Saint-Cloud. What happened to them is what happens when a man and woman are consumed by a flame. Soon they lose any recollection of former pleasure; they forget the limitations of their own bodies, and terms such as "modesty" or "audacity" become equally abstract. The idea of having to part in an hour or two seemed revoltingly immoral. They knew already that a gesture of the other could never be embarrassing; they rediscovered, whispered the crude, awkward, simple words of physical love, pride, gratitude for pleasure given, received. They knew, too, that this moment was exceptional in their lives and that nothing better could be afforded a human being than the discovery of his complement. Unplanned, but now inescapable, physical passion had turned what might have been a passing fancy into a real love affair.

The sky darkened; Lucile and Antoine refused to look at the clock. They smoked, heads thrown back, in an odor of love, battle, and perspiration that they breathed in together like two exhausted, but victorious, warriors. The sheets lay on the floor, Antoine's hand on Lucile's hip.

"I'll never be able to meet you without blushing," said Lucile, "or see you leave without feeling pain, or speak to you in public without turning my eyes away."

She leaned on her elbow, looked at the disorderly room with its narrow window. Antoine laid his hand on her shoulder: she had a very straight, smooth back; ten years and a whole lifetime separated her from Diane. As she turned, he closed his fingers and held the lower part of her face, almost fiercely for a second, her mouth pressed to his palm. Gazing at each other, they wordlessly promised to have thousands of such moments together, no matter what happened.

8

"Don't look so glum, my dear fellow," said Johnny. "This is a cocktail party, not a horror film."

As Johnny slipped a drink into his hand, Antoine smiled mechanically without taking his eyes from the door. They had been there for an hour; it was nine o'clock and no Lucile. What was she doing? She had promised to come. He remembered her voice as she said, "Tomorrow, tomorrow," on his threshold. He had not seen her since. Maybe she was trifling with him. After all, she was maintained by

Blassans-Lignières's generosity; she was a kept woman; she could find young males like himself anywhere. Perhaps yesterday afternoon was only a dream; perhaps, to her, it was nothing more than an afternoon like many others spent with a young man. Perhaps he was idiotic and pretentious. Diane sailed toward him, accompanied by their host, an American "mad about books."

"William, you know Antoine," she said emphatically (as though it was inconceivable that anyone should not know Antoine to be her lover).

"Why, of course," said William, with an appraising smile.

I wonder if he's going to open my mouth and examine my teeth, thought Antoine furiously.

"William has been telling me the most amazing things about Scott Fitzgerald," continued Diane. "He was one of his father's friends. Antoine has a passion for Fitzgerald. You must tell him everything, William, absolutely everything . . ."

The rest of her sentence was lost on Antoine. Lucile came in. She glanced about the drawing room hurriedly, and Antoine understood Johnny's comment of a moment before; she looked terrified, just as he had looked, doubtless, five minutes earlier. She saw him, stopped, and automatically he took a step toward her. A dizziness overcame Antoine: I shall go to her, put my arms around her, kiss her on the mouth; I don't care about the others. Lucile guessed his intention and, for a second, almost let him carry it out. The night, the day had been too long; waiting for Charles had been too long, so that for two hours she had been afraid of arriving at the party to find that Antoine was gone. They stood face to face, dead still, and brusquely Lucile turned away; turned away with a violent movement, exasperated with her own weakness. She could not do it; she tried to think that it was to spare Charles's feelings but she knew that fear was actually the reason.

Johnny stood near her. He smiled and looked at her with a kind of strange concern. She returned his smile, and he took her by the arm to lead her to the buffet.

"You frightened me," he said.

"Why?"

She looked at him squarely. It could not begin already, not so soon: the accomplices, friends, busybodies, sneers. Johnny shrugged his shoulders.

"I'm fond of you," he said gently. "Not that you care, but I'm fond of you."

Somehow his voice moved Lucile. She stared at him. He must be very lonely.

"Why shouldn't I care?"

"Because you're only interested in things that please you. Everything else upsets you. Isn't it so? Anyway, it's not a bad thing in our small set. You'll stay in one piece a little longer."

She listened to him without hearing a word. Antoine had disappeared behind a forest of heads at the other end of the drawing room. Where was he? Where are you, my idiot, my lover? Antoine, where have you hidden your tall, bony frame? Why do you have eyes, so yellow, if you can't see me, here, just ten yards from you, my idiot, my dear idiot? and a feeling of gentleness came over her. What was Johnny saying? It was obvious that she cared only for things that pleased her, and Antoine pleased her. It seemed that, for the first time in years, she was faced with the evidence.

Johnny regarded this evidence with a mixture of envy and sadness. It was true that he liked Lucile, liked the way she kept silent, the way she looked bored, the way she laughed. And now he studied this new face of hers, younger, childlike, almost wild from wanting, and he remembered having wanted like that, long ago, wanting someone more than anything in the world. It was Roger. Yes, he had seen Roger enter as Lucile had done, a drawing room, and he had known the feeling of being dead, or of having returned to life at last. What was real, what was dreamed in these love affairs? Anyway, Antoine had not wasted any time. It was only the day before that he had asked for Lucile's telephone number. Calmly, like an ordinary question, man to man. Curiously, there was a sort of masculine complicity in their relations, and it had not even occurred to Johnny to mention the telephone call to Claire, to whom he usually told everything. There were still some things that Johnny would not do, and Heaven knows, life was expensive.

Diane had not noticed Antoine's behavior, her dress having miraculously hooked on a table at the very moment Lucile entered, and only William was surprised at the young man's flight when Scott Fitzgerald's name was mentioned. Meanwhile, Antoine had rejoined them and was now helping Diane extricate her dress, not without the loss of some beading.

"Your hands are shaking," whispered Diane.

She usually said *vous* to him in public; now she used the more intimate *tu,* as if by accident, but these accidents happened a little too frequently. Antoine resented it. He resented everything about her during the past two days. He resented her sleep, her voice, her elegance, her gestures, the mere fact of her being alive, for being nothing more to him than a way of being invited to the same parties as Lucile. He resented, too, the fact that he had been unable to touch her since. She had become worried immediately. In their physical relations Antoine had always behaved with that perfect regularity resulting from a mixture of sensuality

47

and indifference. He was unaware that this failing on his part gave Diane a little hope, so frightened was she at times of this lover, silent, efficient, and unlyrical. Passion feeds on everything, even what seems to be the most contrary to its yearnings. Meanwhile, Antoine's eyes searched for Lucile. He knew she was there; he watched the door as attentively for fear of her leaving as he had when hoping for her appearance. Blassans-Lignières's voice startled him and he turned, cordially shook hands with Lucile, then with Charles. He met Lucile's eyes once more, and a sense of triumph, of perfect happiness overwhelmed him with such violence that he began to cough in order to conceal his expression.

"Diane," said Blassans-Lignières, "the Boldini I was telling you about belongs to William. You must show it to her, William."

Antoine's glance crossed his as Charles moved away, flanked by Diane and William. The look in Charles's blue eyes was anxious, honest. Was he unhappy? Did he suspect something? Antoine had not thought about Charles. He had concerned himself with Diane, and very little, at that. Since Sarah's death he had never questioned himself about anyone. Now he found himself alone, facing Lucile, and he mutely asked her: Who are you? What do you want of me? What are you doing here? What am I to you?

"I thought I would never get here," said Lucile.

I know nothing about him, she thought, nothing except the way he makes love. What has stirred us to such a degree of passion? It's the fault of others. If we were free, unobserved, surely we should be calmer, less hot-blooded. For an instant, she felt tempted to turn her back on him and join the small group in quest of the Boldini. What kind of future awaited her, with its lies and hasty meetings? She took the cigarette that Antoine offered, and she laid her hand on his. She immediately recognized the warmth, the contact of this hand, and closed her eyes, twice, as though in secret agreement with herself.

"You'll come tomorrow?" asked Antoine hurriedly. "At the same time?"

It seemed to him that he would not have a moment's rest until he knew exactly when he would be holding her in his arms again. She said yes. And like an ebbing tide, apprehension left Antoine, and he even asked himself if their appointment was really that important to him. Yet he had read enough to know that anxiety—perhaps more deeply than jealousy—is love's great accelerator. And, too, he was certain that he had only to offer his hand, to hold Lucile close to him in the middle of the drawing room for the scandal to be bared, the irreparable accomplished; and this very certainty prevented him from making a move, and gave him an ambiguous, but keen, pleasure that he had rarely experienced: dissimulation.

"Well, children, what have you done with your friends?"

Claire's ringing voice made them jump. She placed a hand on Lucile's shoulder and looked appraisingly at Antoine, as though trying to put herself in Lucile's place, and succeeding well. Here comes the feminine-conspirator act, thought Lucile, and to her own surprise, did not feel in the least annoyed. It was true, Antoine was handsome now, his expression troubled, but determined. He was surely too absentminded to succeed in lying for long; he was made for reading, long walks, lovemaking, for silence and not for social life. Even less so than she was: indifference and detachment provided her with an ideal diving suit for the abysmal waters that surrounded her.

"There's a Boldini somewhere belonging to the one they call William," said Antoine waggishly. "Diane and Charles are contemplating it."

49

He reflected that this was the first time he had called Blassans-Lignières by his Christian name. For some unknown reason, deceiving a man led to a certain degree of familiarity.

Claire gave a small cry. "A Boldini? It's new, isn't it? Where did William find it? I didn't know about it," she added in the vexed tone she adopted when a fault was discovered in her network of information. "Poor William must have been swindled, as usual; no one but an American would buy a Boldini without consulting Santos."

Calmed a little by the thought of poor William's imprudence, she turned her attention to Lucile. Perhaps the time had come at last to make this little upstart pay for her insolence, her silence, her refusal to play the game. Lucile smiled, her eyes raised to Antoine, and it was an easy smile, amused and reassured. That was the right term, "reassured." The kind of smile a woman could only have if she knew a man intimately. But when, when could they have met? Claire's mind began to function at top speed. Let's see, the supper at Marnes was three days ago; nothing existed then. It must have been some afternoon; in Paris no one makes love in the evening any more, everyone is too tired. What's more, they have Charles and Diane to cope with. Today? She looked at them, her eyes shining, nostrils flared, trying to detect the traces of pleasure on them with the passionate interest that curiosity gives some women. Lucile understood and, in spite of herself, burst out laughing. Claire withdrew slightly, her fox-hound expression changed into something softer, more resigned, the "all-understood, all-permitted" look, which passed without being noticed, unfortunately.

For Antoine was looking at Lucile, laughing confidentially with her, delighted to hear her laugh, delighted to know that she would tell him why next day in his bed, during the happy, weary period that follows lovemaking. So at present he did not ask "What are you laughing about?" Many affairs are denounced in this way: by silence, the lack of questions, phrases left dangling, a password so commonplace as to become extravagant. In any case, a person who had heard Lucile and Antoine laugh, who had seen their expressions, could not be misled. They themselves felt this vaguely and took a sort of pride in seizing the opportunity offered by the Boldini incident to laugh together without causing alarm. Though they would never have admitted it, the presence of Claire and the other guests increased their pleasure. They felt young, almost like children who have been forbidden to do something, have done it just the same and not yet been punished.

Diane returned, cutting through the crowd, rapidly withdrawing her hand from a friend as he kissed it, neglecting to answer some question about her health or an enthusiastic remark praising her beauty. In a confused murmur of "How are you, Diane? You're in wonderful shape, Diane. Where did you get that divine dress?" she endeavored to reach the dark, malevolent corner where she had left her lover, her true love, with a girl who intrigued him. She hated Charles for having dragged her away from the drawing room; she hated Boldini; she hated William for having recounted that deadly, interminable story about his purchase. He had bought it for a song, of course; it was a great bargain, and the wretched dealer had been completely hoodwinked. It was irritating, this mania that the ultrarich had for always, always getting the better part of an affair. To have a rebate from the dressmaker, a discount at Cartier's, and to be proud of it. She had escaped all that, thank Heaven; she was not one of the women of means who haggled with tradespeople. She must tell that to Antoine, it would amuse him. People amused him; he always quoted Proust on the subject, and on many others as well, which annoyed Diane somewhat, for she had very little time to read. Dear Lucile had certainly read Proust; she looked just the type and, of course, living with Charles, she must have plenty of time. Diane paused. My God, she thought suddenly, I'm being vulgar. Really, can't one grow old without becoming vulgar? Her heart ached. She smiled at Coco de Balileul, returned Maxine's mysterious wink, stumbled over a dozen smiling, friendly obstacles. She accomplished this nightmarish steeplechase to rejoin Antoine, who was laughing over there, laughing in his deep voice; she must stop that laugh. She took another step and closed her eyes with relief: he was laughing with Claire Santré. Lucile had her back turned to them.

9

"What a noisy party," said Charles. "People drink more and more, don't they?"

The car glided gently over the quays; it was raining. As usual, Lucile had leaned her head on the edge of the window; little raindrops sprinkled her face. She breathed in the smell of Paris, the April night, and thought of Antoine's tormented face when they had been obliged to say good-bye, half an hour earlier. Everything seemed wonderful.

"People are more and more frightened," she replied gaily. "Frightened of growing old, of losing what they have, of not being able to get what they want, of being bored, they live in a constant state of panic and greed."

"That amuses you?" asked Charles.

"It amuses me sometimes, and sometimes it touches me. Doesn't it you?"

"I pay very little attention," said Charles. "As you know, I'm not much of a psychologist. All I notice is that more and more strangers fall into my arms and more and more of them stagger about drawing rooms."

He could not say: I'm only interested in you; I spend hours and hours prying into the workings of your mind. I am tormented by an *idée fixe*. I too am frightened, as you say: frightened of losing what I have. I too live in a constant state of panic and greed.

Lucile drew in her head and looked at him. She was filled with tenderness; she had never been fonder of him. She would have liked to share with him the wild happiness she felt in thinking of the next day: It's ten o'clock, only seventeen hours before I'll be in Antoine's arms. If only I can sleep late, the time will pass without my noticing it. She laid her hand on Charles's. His was a fine, well-kept hand, with a few small yellow spots that had begun to appear.

"How was the Boldini?"

She's trying to please me, thought Charles bitterly. She knows that I'm a man of taste as well as a businessman. She doesn't know that I'm fifty and wretchedly unhappy.

"Rather pretty. In his best manner. William bought it for next to nothing."

"William always gets everything for next to nothing." Lucile laughed.

"That's exactly the reflection of Diane," answered Charles.

There was a vague pause. I'm not going to be silent with embarrassment whenever he mentions Diane or Antoine, thought Lucile. It's too silly. If only I could tell him the truth: I'm very much taken with Antoine; I feel like laughing with him, to be in his arms. What more dreadful thing could I say to a man who loves me? He might, perhaps, put up with my sleeping with Antoine, but not to my laughing with him. I know: to jealousy, nothing is more frightful than laughter.

"Diane looked so strange," she said. "I was talking to Claire and Antoine when she returned to the drawing room. Her face was tense, her expression searching . . . she frightened me."

She tried to laugh. Charles turned to her.

"Frightened? You mean that you felt sorry for her?"

"Yes," she said quietly. "I felt sorry for her, too. Growing old is no joke for a woman."

"Or for a man," replied Charles briskly. "I can guarantee that."

They laughed, a laugh that rang false and chilled their blood. So that's the way it is, thought Lucile. Very well, we'll avoid the subject; we'll joke and do whatever pleases him, but tomorrow at five, I'll be in Antoine's arms.

And she who detested ferocity felt delighted to discover that she was capable of it.

For nothing, no one, no amount of pleading could prevent her from meeting Antoine the next day, from knowing once more the body, the breath, the voice of Antoine. She was certain of it, and the relentlessness of her desire, she whose every plan usually depended only on a mood or the weather, surprised her even more than the perfect joy she had felt on meeting Antoine's eyes earlier that evening. Her only love affair, at twenty, had been unfortunate, and she now considered passion with a curious mixture of respect and sadness, approaching what she felt for religion: a lost sentiment. She suddenly discovered love in all its force—requited, happy love—and it seemed as though her life, instead of being confined to one being, became immense, impossible to fill, triumphal. She, whose days passed nonchalantly, without a landmark, felt alarmed to see how little of life remained to her: she would never have enough time to love Antoine.

"As you know, Lucile, I must go to New York soon. Would you come with me?"

Charles's voice was quiet and intimated that she would agree. He knew that Lucile was fond of traveling. She did not answer at once.

"Why not? Will you be there long?"

Impossible, she thought. Impossible. How can I do without Antoine for ten days? Charles imposed his terms too early or too late and, in any case, too cruelly. I'd give all the cities in the world for Antoine's room. I have no other journeys, no other discoveries to make except those we can make together in the dark. And as a precise detail returned suddenly in her memory, she was troubled and turned her head toward the street.

"Ten or fifteen days," said Charles. "New York is charming in the spring. You've only been there in midwinter. I remember the cold was so intense that your nose turned blue; you stared, your hair bristled with indignation, and you glared at me as though it were my fault."

He began to laugh, his voice soft, melancholic. Lucile remembered the abominable cold of that winter, but nothing else. She had not a single fond memory. Simply racing wildly in a taxi from the hotel to a restaurant. The golden memories belonged to Charles, always to Charles, and suddenly she felt ashamed. Sentimentally, too, she depended on Charles, and that was more embarrassing than the rest. She did not wish to hurt him; she did not wish to

55

lie to him; she did not wish to tell him the truth; she simply wished to let him guess it, without explanations. Yes, she was really the perfect coward.

They met two or three times a week. Antoine found many imaginative excuses for leaving his office, and Lucile did not tell Charles how she spent her days; she never had. They joined each other in the little room and, trembling, they sank into darkness; they scarcely had time to speak. They knew nothing about one another, but their bodies showed recognition with such fervor, respect, such a feeling for the absolute, that their memories disconnected under the impact; on parting, they searched desperately, and in vain, for one among the words whispered in the dark, for a single clear recollection. They always parted like two somnambulists, almost distracted, and it was only an hour or two later that they began to await the only reality, the only vital point in their lives: the moment when they would meet again. All the rest was dead. This expectancy was the only thing that made them aware of time, the weather, and other people, because it transformed these things into obstacles. Lucile would make sure, six times at least, before meeting Antoine, that the car keys were in her handbag, remind herself a dozen times which streets led to Antoine's house, look a dozen times at the alarm clock that she had always so proudly disdained. Antoine reminded his secretary that he had an urgent appointment at four, and left the office fifteen minutes before, although his room was two minutes away. And they arrived each time a little pale, Lucile, because she had thought that a bottleneck in the traffic would prevent her from arriving on time, and Antoine, because one of his firm's authors had stopped by and kept him an unwilling prisoner. Sighing, they clung to each other, as though they had escaped a great danger which, at worst, would have meant a five-minute delay.

During an embrace, they said "I love you," but never otherwise. Sometimes Antoine bent over Lucile and, as she caught her breath, her eyes closed, he outlined her face, her shoulder with his hand, saying tenderly, "You make me very happy, you know." She smiled. He talked about her smile, told her how annoyed he was when she smiled, her eyes wide, at someone else. "Your smile is too disarming," he said, "it worries me."—"But I'm often thinking of other things; it's just a way of being agreeable. I don't look disarming, I look vacant."—"Heaven knows what you think about," he continued. "At dinner parties you always seem to be brooding over a secret or some low blow."—"Antoine, I do brood over a secret. . . ." and she laid her head on his shoulder, whispering: "Don't brood over things too much, Antoine; we're all right." He would become silent; he dared not tell her what was unceasingly on his mind, what kept him awake during those long nights with Diane, who also pretended to be asleep: This can't go on; really it can't go on. Why isn't Lucile with me? This unconcern, Lucile's capacity to waive all problems, made him uneasy. She refused to talk about Charles, she refused any plans. Had she, perhaps, bound herself to Blassans-Lignières for selfish reasons? But she seemed so free, avoided so naturally any discussion the moment it turned to money (and Heaven knows that nobody talks so much about money as those who have too much of it), that he could not imagine her doing anything calculated. She said, "I have a taste for facility." She said, "I hate the instinct of possession." She also said, "I was lonely without you." And he found all this difficult to reconcile. He waited, confused, for some-

57

thing to happen, for someone to ferret them out, for fate to take over his responsibilities as a man, and he despised himself.

Antoine knew that he was indolent, sensual but moral. No woman had ever attracted him so much as Lucile, but he had had numerous love affairs, and remorse had turned his rather insignificant liaison with Sarah into a tragic love story. He knew himself to be prone to inner conflicts. In fact, he had almost as great a capacity for misfortune as for happiness, and Lucile could only upset him. He did not understand that she had only loved once, ten years earlier, had forgotten all about it, and considered their present love as a marvelous, unexpected, fragile, and unhoped-for gift of which she superstitiously refused to foresee the consequences. She liked waiting for him, longing for him; she liked their hidden meetings as much as she would have liked to live with him openly. Every moment of happiness was sufficient in itself. And if, for the last two months, she was surprised at her susceptibility to adolescent love songs, she never felt personally concerned by the "you and only you, for ever and ever" that was the usual theme. As her only form of morality was the avoidance of self-deceit, she was naturally drawn into a profound but involuntary cynicism. It seemed as though the fact of being able to sort out one's feelings automatically led to this cynicism, while cheats and liars could remain wildly romantic all their lives. She loved Antoine, but cared for Charles; Antoine made her happy, and she did not make Charles unhappy. As she valued both men, she was not sufficiently interested in herself to be ashamed of allowing herself to be shared by both. Her total lack of self-sufficiency made her ruthless; in short, she was happy.

It was quite by chance that she discovered she could suffer.

She had not seen Antoine for three days, for chance had invited them to different theaters and dinners. She was to meet him at four o'clock and she arrived on time, surprised not to find him at his door. For the first time, she used the key he had given her. The room was empty and the blinds open. For a moment she thought she had made a mistake, as she had always arrived to find a darkened room, Antoine lighting only a lamp that stood on the floor, one that lit up the bed and a corner of the ceiling. Amused, she walked about the room she knew so well and yet so little, reading the titles of books on the shelves, picking up a tie on the carpet, examining a charmingly absurd 1900 painting that she had never noticed. For the first time, she imagined her lover as a young bachelor of modest means who worked from time to time. Who was Antoine? Where did he come from? Who were his parents? What had been his childhood? She sat down on the bed, then, suddenly nervous, rose and went to the window. She felt that she was in a stranger's room, her presence there indiscreet. And above all, and for the first time, she thought of Antoine as "someone else," and that what she knew of his hands, mouth, and eyes did not necessarily make him a permanent accomplice. Where was he? It was a quarter past four; she had not seen him for three days and the telephone did not ring. She wandered about the sad room from door to window, picked up a book, could not understand a word of what she read, put it down again. Time went by; he should have telephoned if something had detained him. She took up the receiver, hoping the line was out of order, but it was not. And if he had not felt like keeping the appointment? The idea froze her motionless in the middle of the room, attentive, like certain mortally wounded soldiers seen in old prints. A storm broke loose in her memory: what she had taken for disapproval in Antoine's eyes was boredom; his hesitation when she had once asked him what worried him was not the fear of being contrary, but the fear of making her suffer by admitting the truth: he was no longer in love with her. A dozen of Antoine's attitudes passed through her mind in a flash, and she put them all down to indifference. She said aloud: "Well, that's that. He doesn't love me any longer." She said the words in a quiet voice, and immediately the sentence returned to her like a whiplash; her hand went to her throat as if in defense: "But what am I to do with myself if Antoine doesn't love me any more?" Her life seemed drained of blood, bereft of warmth and gaiety, like the petrified, cinder-covered plain in Peru, a photograph of which had recently appeared in *Match,* much to Antoine's rather morbid admiration.

She remained standing, shaking so violently that she came to her own rescue: "Come, come," she said aloud, "come now . . ." She spoke to her heart and body as though they were a team of terrified horses, then lay down on the bed, forcing herself to breathe quietly. In vain. A kind of panic of despair crumpled her; both hands grasping her shoulders, face buried in the pillow, she heard her own voice moan, "Antoine, Antoine . . ." and with the unbearable pain came an equally great amazement. "You're crazy," she said to herself, "crazy." But someone who was not herself and who, for once, was stronger than she, cried out, "And Antoine's golden eyes, and Antoine's voice—what can you do without Antoine, you fool?" A church clock struck five, and she imagined that some cruel, mad god was tolling the hour for her. A second later, Antoine appeared. He paused when he saw her expression, then dropped down beside her on the bed. He was mad with happiness; he covered her face, her hair with gentle kisses; he explained, he showered insults on his publisher, who had detained him at the office for an hour. Whispering his name in a broken voice she clung to him, then, sitting up, turned away.

"Antoine," she said, "I love you for keeps."

"That's good," he answered. "Because I love you, too."

They kept a thoughtful silence. Then she turned to him, and she looked gravely at the face she loved as it drew close to hers.

10

When she left him, two hours later, Lucile thought her anxiety had been accidental. Brimming over with joy, exhausted by love, empty-headed, she believed that those thirty minutes of panic were due to a nervous rather than to a sentimental cause, and decided to sleep more, drink less, et cetera. Being so accustomed to an intensely solitary life, she could not easily admit that something or someone might be indispensable to her. It seemed, in fact, even more monstrous than desirable. Her car moved quietly along the Seine; she drove mechanically, admiring the aspect of the shimmering river on one of the first fine spring evenings. She smiled faintly. What had come over her? At her age? With the life she led? After all, she was a kept woman, a cynic. The idea made her laugh, and the man in the car next to hers smiled at her. She returned his smile absently and went on musing. Yes, who was she? She was completely indifferent as to how she appeared in other people's eyes and, until now, in her own. She no longer saw herself. Was that bad? Was it a sign of mental debasement? She had been an avid reader when younger, before discovering that she was happy. She had asked herself many questions before becoming this well-fed and svelte animal that avoided all complications with such agility. Because of the strange line of life in her palm, she had always nonchalantly admitted that she would die young; she even counted on it. But if she lived to be old? She tried to imagine herself aged, poor, deserted by Charles, laboring at some menial trade. She tried to frighten herself, but she did not succeed. At the same time, she thought that no matter what happened, the Seine would always look as luminous and golden near the Grand Palais, and that was the most important thing. To live, she did not need this purring car, or her coat from Laroche—of that she was certain. Charles knew it, too, which made him unhappy. And, as happened every time she left Antoine, she felt a surge of tenderness for Blassans-Lignières and a deep desire to make him happy.

She did not know that Charles, who usually found her at home when he returned from his office, was pacing up and down his room, as she had done three hours earlier, asking himself the same question: "And if she never came back?" She did not know it and she would never know, for when she came in he was lying on his bed, placidly reading *Le Monde*. He always recognized the sound of her car. "Had a nice day?" he inquired, and she kissed him softly. She liked the scent he used; she must remember to buy some for Antoine.

"Very nice," she answered, "but I was afraid of . . ."

She stopped. She wanted to talk to Charles, to tell him everything, "I was afraid of losing Antoine, afraid of loving him." But she could not; there was no one to whom she could talk about her strange afternoon. She had never savored confidences, and this made her feel a little sad.

"I was afraid of living on the edges," she added with confusion.

"On the edges of what?"

"Life. What others call life. Charles, must one really love, I mean, have an unfortunate love affair, must one work, do things in order to exist?"

"It's not absolutely necessary," he said (he lowered his eyes), "as long as you are happy."

"And that seems enough to you?"

"By far." And something in his voice, a strange, faraway melancholy tore Lucile's heart.

She sat on the bed, reached out her hand, caressed his weary face. Charles closed his eyes, smiled faintly. She felt understanding, good, capable of charity, but she did not admit that she owed these noble sentiments to Antoine's arrival and that if he had not come she would have detested Charles. When one is happy it is easy to accept others as accomplices in this happiness, and it is only after they have gone that one knows them to have been but insignificant witnesses.

"What are we doing tonight?" she asked.

"There's Diane's dinner," said Charles. "Have you forgotten about it?"

His voice was incredulous but delighted. She guessed why, and blushed. If she had answered yes, it would be true and yet, at the same time, mislead him. She really could not say: "I had forgotten the dinner, but not Antoine. I've just been with him. We were both in such a bewildered state that we forgot about seeing each other tonight and made an appointment for tomorrow."

"I hadn't forgotten it," she replied, "but I didn't know if the dinner was to be at her house. What dress would you like me to wear?"

She felt surprised not to be more pleased at the thought of seeing Antoine again in a few hours. On the contrary, she was vaguely annoyed. They had reached such a pitch of emotion that afternoon that it seemed, if the term could be applied to sentiment, that her cup was brimming over. She would have preferred dining quietly with Charles. She opened her mouth to say so, but stopped: it would give him too much pleasure, a false pleasure, and she did not want to lie to him.

"What were you going to say?"

"I don't remember."

"Your metaphysical reflections make you look even more muddled than usual."

"Do I usually look muddled?" she asked, laughing.

"Very. I would never dare allow you to travel alone, for instance. A week later, I should find you in a waiting room, Lord knows where, surrounded by stacks of pocket books, with a thorough knowledge of the barmen's lives."

He seemed almost worried by such a possibility, and she burst out laughing. He really considered her incapable of coping with life and, in a flash, she realized that this was what attached him to her, far more than any feeling of security. He accepted her irresponsibility; he confirmed the choice she had unconsciously made, fifteen years earlier, never to quit her adolescence. The same decision that probably exasperated Antoine. And, perhaps, the character she wanted to be and the one Charles imagined agreed so perfectly that this would prove more powerful than any love that might force her to disown them.

"Meanwhile, let's have a drink," said Charles. "I'm dead tired."

"Pauline doesn't want me to drink," said Lucile. "Ask her for a double whisky and I'll have some out of your glass."

Charles smiled and rang for Pauline. I'm beginning to act like a little girl, thought Lucile, almost in spite of myself, and before long I'll have a collection of plush animals on my bed. She stretched, went to her room and, looking at her bed, wondered if one day she would wake up with Antoine by her side.

11

Diane's flat on the Rue Cambon was lovely, filled with flowers, and, in spite of the mild weather, and the opened French windows, two large wood fires blazed in hearths at either end of the drawing room. A delighted Lucile at one moment breathed in the smell from the street that already announced the approaching summer, a languid, dusty, hot summer, and at another moment the burning logs that recalled last autumn's bitter cold, linked forever in her mind with the woods in Sologne where Charles had taken her hunting.

"How wonderful," she said to Diane, "to have combined two seasons in a single evening."

"Yes," said Diane, "but it gives one the feeling of wearing the wrong clothes."

Lucile began to laugh. She had a quiet, infectious laugh; she spoke without a shade of constraint, and Diane wondered if her own jealousy was not absurd. All things considered, Lucile behaved well; of course, she had that absentminded, vague attitude that recalled Antoine, but perhaps that was their only affinity. Blassans-Lignières seemed relaxed; Antoine had never been in such good humor; surely she must be mistaken. She made a gesture of friendliness, almost of gratitude toward Lucile.

"Come with me, I'll show you the rest of the flat. Would it amuse you?"

Lucile gravely inspected a bathroom tiled with Italian ceramics, admired the convenient wardrobes, and followed Diane into her bedroom.

"It's rather a mess," said Diane. "Don't look at it too closely."

Antoine had come in late and changed for dinner in her room. The shirt and tie he had worn that afternoon lay on the floor. Diane glanced quickly at Lucile and detected nothing more than a faint sign of disapproval. But something urged Diane, something she was ashamed of and yet could not repress, to pick up his clothing, put them on an armchair, and then face Lucile with a little smile of complicity.

"Men are so untidy." She looked Lucile in the eye.

"Charles is very neat," replied Lucile affably.

She wanted to laugh. What next? she thought. Is she going to explain that Antoine never replaces the cap on his tube of toothpaste? She felt no jealousy; the tie had appeared to her like an old school friend met by some miracle at the foot of the Pyramids. At the same time, she thought Diane very beautiful and that it was strange that Antoine should neglect such beauty for her sake. She felt objective, astute, and benevolent, as she always did after drinking a little too much.

"We must go back to the guests," said Diane. "I don't know why I feel obliged to give parties from time to time. It's exhausting for a hostess, and I don't believe people enjoy themselves much."

"The party seems very gay," said Lucile with conviction. "Anyway, Claire is pouting a little, which is always a good sign."

"So you've noticed that?" Diane smiled. "I shouldn't have thought it of you. You always seem a trifle . . . er . . ."

66

"Muddled," said Lucile.

"That's it, exactly."

"Charles told me the same thing this evening at seven o'clock. I shall soon believe it's true."

They both laughed, and Lucile suddenly felt a certain affection for Diane. In their little group, she was one of the few women to possess a little moral distinction; she had never heard her make a low or commonplace remark. Charles spoke well of her and he was extremely particular regarding a generally prevalent form of vulgarity. It was a pity not to be able to make a friend of her. Perhaps someday, if Diane were really intelligent, everything could be settled for the best. Lucile mistook her own crazy optimism for wisdom, and if Antoine had not come in at that moment nothing would have prevented her from beginning an explanation to Diane that could only have proved disastrous.

"Destret is looking for you everywhere," said Antoine. "He's furious." Troubled, he looked at Diane and Lucile.

He must imagine that I'm jealous and searching for proof, thought Diane, reassured by Lucile's unmistakable gaiety. Poor Antoine . . .

"We weren't up to anything; I was just showing Lucile the flat. She had never seen it."

And Lucile, amused by Antoine's confused expression, laughed with her. They gave the impression of conspiracy, and a masculine anger flared up in Antoine: What! I've just left the arms of one; I'm going to sleep with the other, and together they're making fun of me! It's really too much!

"Just what did I say that was so funny?" he asked.

"But not a thing," answered Diane. "You seem to show an elaborate concern for Destret's bad temper, when you know as well as I that he's always in a rage. It amuses us, that's all."

She walked out first and Lucile followed, making a contemptuous and disgusted grimace for Antoine's benefit. He hesitated, then smiled. She had said "I love you for keeps" only two hours earlier, and he remembered her voice when she said it. She could be as impertinent as she pleased now.

In the drawing room, Lucile fell upon Johnny, who was feeling bored and, consequently, hurried up to her with a drink and guided her toward the window.

"I adore you, Lucile," he said. "With you, at least, I'm at ease. I know you won't tell me what you think of the guests' morals or rant about the latest play."

"You tell me that every time."

"Be careful," he said brusquely. "You look insolently happy."

She absently ran her hand over her face, as though happiness were a mask that she had forgotten to remove. For indeed, that day she had said "I love you" to someone who had answered "I do, too." Did it show so much? All of a sudden, she felt that she was the center of attraction, that every eye was fixed on her. She blushed, gulped down the almost undiluted whisky that Johnny had given her.

"It's just that I'm in a good humor," she said feebly, "and think these people are charming."

And she, who so seldom made an effort at parties, suddenly decided to apologize for her beaming face, just as certainly ugly women talk unceasingly in order to make people forget their plainness. Lucile went from group to group, amiably, confused, going so far as to congratulate the astonished Claire on her wonderful dress. Charles's eyes followed her, intrigued, and he had almost decided to take her home when Diane took him by the arm.

"This is the first nice evening of spring, Charles. We're

going dancing. No one feels sleepy, and Lucile least of all."

She gave Lucile a kindly, amused glance, and Charles, who knew her jealousy and who, besides, had seen her draw Lucile aside for a few minutes, suddenly felt reassured. Lucile must have forgotten Antoine. And without saying so, it was a sort of gala, a festivity in honor of peace, that Diane had offered him. He accepted.

They were all to meet in a nightclub. Charles and Lucile were the first to appear; they danced, they talked gaily, for Lucile, once started, chattered like a magpie. All of a sudden she stopped. She saw in the doorway a tall man, a little taller than the others, in a dark blue suit, and his eyes were yellow. She knew that man's face by heart, every scar under the dark blue suit, and the shape of his shoulders. He came up to them and sat down. Diane was downstairs making up her face, and he asked Lucile to dance. The pressure of his hand on her shoulder, the touch of his palm against hers, and the strange distance he kept between his cheek and Lucile's, a distance that Lucile recognized to be that of desire, stirred her so deeply that she even pretended to look slightly bored in order to deceive a public that took no notice of her. This was the first time that she had danced with Antoine, and they danced to one of the lilting, sentimental tunes played everywhere that spring.

He took her back to her table. Diane had returned and was dancing with Charles. They sat on the banquette, at some distance from each other.

"Did you have a nice time?" Antoine asked, looking furious.

"Why, yes," answered Lucile, surprised. "Didn't you?"

"Not at all," he said. "I never have a good time at that sort of party and, unlike you, I have a horror of false situations."

The truth was that he had been unable to talk to Lucile

during the whole evening, and he wanted her. The idea that she would leave with Charles in a few minutes filled him with bitterness. He lapsed into a kind of virtuous exclusiveness that is so often caused by frustrated desire.

"You're made for this sort of life," he said.

"What about you?"

"I'm not. Some men exhibit their virility by navigating between two women. My virility prevents me from having pleasure in making them suffer."

"If you had seen yourself in Diane's room!" exclaimed Lucile. "You looked so sheepish . . ."

She began to laugh.

"Don't laugh," said Antoine, controlling his voice. "In ten minutes you'll be in Charles's arms, or alone. In either case, far from me . . ."

"But tomorrow . . ."

"I've had enough of tomorrows," he replied. "You must understand that."

Lucile was silent. She tried unsuccessfully to look grave. Alcohol made her feel unreasonably happy. An unknown young man asked her to dance, but Antoine curtly sent him away, much to her annoyance. She would have been glad to dance, talk, or even run away with someone else; she felt freed of every obligation, except that of enjoying herself.

"I've had a little too much to drink," she said plaintively.

"That's obvious," answered Antoine.

"Perhaps you should have done the same; you're surely not amusing."

This was their first quarrel. She looked at his childlike, obstinate profile, and softened.

"Antoine, you know very well—"

"Yes, yes, that you love me for keeps."

And he got up. Diane came back to their table. Charles seemed tired. He gave Lucile an imploring glance and

70

asked Diane to excuse them: he had to be up early the next morning and the place was really too noisy for him. Lucile did not protest, and followed him. But in the car, and for the first time since she had met Charles, she felt like a prisoner.

12

Diane was removing her makeup in the bathroom. Antoine had turned on the phonograph, sat down on the floor, and listened to, without hearing, a Beethoven concerto. Diane saw him in a mirror, and smiled. Antoine always sat in front of the phonograph, as he might have before a pagan image or a wood fire. She had wasted her time in explaining to him that the sound from the new speakers came from both sides of the room, converging in the center on a level with her bed; he always settled down in front of the apparatus, as though fascinated by the record's black, shining rotation. She carefully took off her daytime makeup, then applied another for the night, specially prepared to conceal wrinkles without deepening them. It was out of the question to let her skin breathe (as advised by women's magazines) any more than she could allow her heart to breathe. She hadn't the time now. She considered her beauty indispensable in holding Antoine, and for that reason she did not try to save it for a future without interest. Some characters, the most generous ones, concentrate only on the present, and burn the rest. Diane was among them.

Antoine stiffened as he heard faint noises in the bathroom: the tearing Kleenex and the swish of a hairbrush more than covered the violins and brasses of the concerto. Another five minutes and he would have to get up, undress, and slip into those so soft sheets, next to that so exquisitely groomed woman, in this so lovely room. But he wanted Lucile. Lucile had come to his room and fallen on the landlady's rickety bed; Lucile had undressed at top speed and vanished as quickly; she was elusive, his little thief, his guest. She would never settle down; he would never wake at her side; she was a transitory being. What was more, he had ruined her evening; he felt his throat tighten with an adolescent despair.

Diane appeared in her blue dressing gown and, for a second, studied the back, the rigid neck that she refused to consider hostile. She was tired; she had, exceptionally, drunk a little, and she was in a good humor. She wanted Antoine to talk to her, laugh with her, tell her about his childhood without holding anything back. She did not know that he was obsessed by dissimulation, by the moral obligation of their lovemaking that he incorrectly thought to be the only thing she wanted of him. So when she sat down and slipped her arm through his in a friendly way, he thought, Yes, yes, just a second, with a mental caddishness that was most unusual in him. For even in his shabbiest adventures, he had always preserved a certain respect for love, like the minute of silence, before laying his hand on a woman.

"I like that concerto," said Diane.

"It's very pretty," agreed Antoine in the polite tone of someone lying on the beach, who has been disturbed by being asked to look at the blue of the Mediterranean.

"The party was quite a success, wasn't it?"

"With all of the fireworks," he replied, and stretched out on the carpet, his eyes closed.

He seemed immense as he lay there, more solitary than ever. He still heard the sarcastic, unkind intonation of his own voice, and hated himself for it. Diane remained motionless, "handsome, old and painted." Where had he read that? Pepys's Diary?

"Were you so bored?" she asked.

She stood up, walked about the room, straightened a flower in a vase, ran her hand fondly over a piece of furniture. He watched her through his lashes. She loved these things, she loved these damned things, and he was one of them, the prize piece of her collection; he was a kept young man. Not really kept, of course, but he dined with "her friends," slept in "her flat," lived "her life." It was easy enough for him to judge Lucile. At least Lucile was a woman.

"Why don't you answer? Were you that bored?"

Her voice. Her questions. Her dressing gown. Her perfume. He could stand it no longer. He rolled over on his stomach, his face in his arms. She knelt by him.

"Antoine . . . Antoine . . ."

There was such desolation, such tenderness in her voice that he turned over. Her eyes were shining a bit too much. Looking away, he drew her to him. Her movement was awkward, frightened, as she lay down by him, as though she were afraid of breaking something or had a touch of rheumatism. And because he did not love Diane, he suddenly wanted her.

Charles had left for New York, alone, the trip reduced to four days. Lucile wandered through the hazy blue streets of Paris in the open car. She awaited summer, recognized its approach in every scent, in every shimmer of the Seine. She imagined already the smell of dust, trees, and earth that would soon invade the Boulevard Saint-Germain, and at night the tall chestnut trees outlined against the pink sky and all but concealing it; the street lamps always lighted too early, their professional pride humbled by

73

changing from valuable guides in winter to summer parasites—squeezed between the lingering nightfall and the dawn already impatient on the horizon. The first evening, she roamed about Saint-Germain-des-Prés, met friends from the university and from later days, who greeted her with shouts as though she were the ghost she soon felt herself to be. After the exchange of a few jokes, a few memories, she realized that their lives were dominated by a profession, money worries, girl friends, and that her own unconcern was more of an annoyance to them than a distraction. One broke through a money barrier as one did through a sound barrier: each spoken word returned a few seconds late, too late, to the speaker.

She declined to dine with them at the old bistro on the Rue Cujas; she went home at eight thirty, a little depressed. An approving Pauline cooked a steak for her in the kitchen, and she lay down on her bed, the window wide open. Night spread rapidly over the carpet; street noises died away, and she remembered the morning wind of two months before. Not a settled, languid wind like the present one, but a brash, swift, and frisky wind that had forced her to get up, just as this one lulled her to sleep. Between the two, there had been Antoine; and life. She was to dine with him next day. Alone, for the first time. It troubled her. She was more afraid of boring than of being bored. But, on the other hand, life was so kind to her, there was such sweetness in lying on her bed gradually being hemmed in by the shadows, she so much approved of the idea that the world was round and life complicated that it was impossible to imagine anything unfortunate happening to her, for any reason.

There are moments of perfect happiness, remembered sometimes in loneliness and more important than any others, that can save you from despair in a crisis. For you know that you have been happy, alone and without reason. You know that it is possible. And happiness—which seems so closely connected with someone who makes you unhappy, so irrevocably, almost organically dependent on this person—reappears to you as a thing smooth, round, intact, free, and in your power (remote, surely, but possible). And this memory is more comforting than that of a happiness shared before, with someone else; for this someone, no longer loving, is seen in error and the happy memory based on nothing.

She was to call for Antoine at six o'clock the next day. They would take Lucile's car and drive to the country for dinner. They would have the whole night to themselves. She fell asleep smiling.

The gravel crunched under the waiters' feet, bats swooped about the terrace lights, and at the next table a congested-looking couple silently devoured an *omelette flambée*. They were about ten miles from Paris; it had turned rather cool, and the proprietress placed a shawl over Lucile's shoulders. The inn was one among a dozen others that more or less guaranteed privacy and fresh air to adulterous or weary Parisians. The wind had ruffled Antoine's hair; he laughed. Lucile told him about her childhood, a happy one.

". . . My father was a notary. He had a passion for La Fontaine. He used to walk along the banks of the Indre reciting his fables. Later, he wrote some himself, changing the characters, of course. I'm surely one of the only women in France who knows by heart a fable called *The Lamb and the Crow*. You're lucky."

"I'm very lucky," said Antoine, "I know it. Go on."

"He died when I was twelve, and my brother was stricken with polio. He is still in a wheelchair. My mother was seized with a devouring passion for him, of course. She never leaves him. She's rather forgotten me, I think."

She paused. When she had come to Paris, she managed, not without difficulty, to send some money to her mother every month. For the past two years, Charles had sent it, without ever mentioning the fact.

"My parents hated each other," said Antoine. "They refused to divorce only so that I might have a home. I would have infinitely preferred to have two, I assure you."

He smiled, reached across the table, and squeezed Lucile's hand.

"Do you realize? We have the whole evening, the whole night."

"We'll go slowly back to Paris with the top down. You'll drive very slowly because it's cold. I'll light your cigarettes so you won't have to take your hands off the wheel."

"We'll go slowly because you want me to. We'll go dancing. Then we'll get into bed, and tomorrow morning you'll know at last whether I take tea or coffee and how much sugar."

"Dancing? We'll run into everyone we know."

"So what?" asked Antoine dryly. "You don't imagine that I'm going to spend my life hiding, do you?"

She looked down, without answering.

"You'll have to make a decision," said Antoine gently. "But not tonight; don't worry."

She raised her head, so obviously relieved that he could not help laughing.

"I already know that the slightest delay enchants you. You only live in the present don't you?"

She did not reply. She was perfectly happy with him, perfectly natural; he made her feel like laughing, talking, making love; he gave her everything, and it frightened her a little.

76

She woke up early the next day, and opened her bewildered eyes to the untidy room and the long arm sprinkled with blond hairs that prevented her from stirring. She shut her eyes immediately, rolled over, smiled. She was next to Antoine, she knew what was meant by the expression "night of love." They had gone dancing and had met no one. Afterward, they had returned to his room and talked, made love, smoked, talked, made love until broad daylight found them in bed, drunk with words and action, in that deep, exhausted peace that follows excesses. They had thought a little of dying that night, in their violence, and sleep had come to them like a marvelous raft on which they had climbed and stretched out before fainting, still holding hands as a last complicity. She looked at Antoine's averted profile, his neck, the stubble on his cheeks, the blue shadows under his eyes, and it was inconceivable to her that she could have ever awakened with anyone else. She was glad to find him so dreamy and nonchalant in the daytime, so violent and precise at night. As though love roused in him a carefree pagan whose one inexorable law was pleasure.

He moved his head, opened his eyes, and gave her the babyish, half-hesitant, half-surprised glance that men have in the morning. He recognized her, and smiled. His head, warm and heavy with sleep, weighed on Lucile's shoulder; she looked amusedly at his big feet sticking out of the tangle of sheets at the other end of the bed. He sighed and muttered something plaintively.

"It's incredible; your eyes are an even paler yellow in the morning," she said. "They look like beer."

"How very poetical you are," he replied.

He sat up quickly, caught Lucile's face, and turned it to the light.

"Yours are almost blue."

"No, they're gray. Grayish-green."

"Braggart."

They sat in bed, face to face, naked. He still held her face in his hand, a searching expression, and they both smiled. His shoulders were very broad and bony; she freed herself and laid her cheek against his body. She listened to his heart beating wildly, as wildly as her own.

"Your heart is thumping," she said. "Are you tired?"

"No," he answered, "it's beating *la chamade.*"

"What is a *chamade,* exactly?"

"You'll have to look it up in the dictionary," he said. "I haven't time to explain now."

And he stretched lazily across the bed. It was broad daylight.

At noon, Antoine telephoned his office, explained that he was feverish but would be there in the afternoon.

"I know it's a schoolboy's excuse, but I don't want to be kicked out. No question of that, it's what's called my daily bread."

"Do you earn much money?" asked Lucile idly.

"Very little," he replied in the same tone. "Do you think that it's important?"

"No, I think that money is convenient, that's all."

"Convenient to the point of being important?"

She looked at him in surprise.

"Why all of these questions?"

"Because I intend to live with you, therefore to support you—"

"Excuse me," interrupted Lucile very quickly, "but I can earn my own living. I worked a year at *L'Appel,* a paper that no longer exists. It was interesting, except that everybody was horribly serious and preachy and—"

Antoine reached out, gagged her.

"You understood me exactly. I want to live with you, or

never see you again. I live here; I make very little money and cannot, in any way, support you on your present scale. Do you hear me?"

"But what about Charles?" asked Lucile feebly.

"It's Charles or I," he said. "Charles is returning home tomorrow, isn't he? Tomorrow night, you come here for good, or we shall see no more of each other. There."

He got up and went to the bathroom. Lucile bit her nails; she tried, unsuccessfully, to think. She stretched and shut her eyes. It was bound to happen, she knew it would happen; men were so horribly tiresome. By the day after tomorrow, she would have to make a decision and, of all the words in the language, that was the one she hated most.

13

Orly was flooded with cold sunshine that reflected on the windows and the silvery backs of the planes, the puddles of water on the landing strip forming thousands of brilliant gray flashes. Charles's flight was two hours late, and Lucile wandered nervously about the main hall. If anything happened to Charles she could not bear it, it would be her fault; she had refused to leave with him and, what was more, she had been unfaithful. And the sad, determined face she wore two hours earlier, a face intended to warn Charles, before she even spoke, that something was wrong, had become anxious and tender. That was the face he saw as he left the customs, and his warm, comforting smile brought tears to Lucile's eyes. He came up to her, kissed her fondly, held her tightly for a moment, and Lucile saw a young woman give her a hard, jealous look. She always forgot that Charles was handsome, because his tenderness for her was so exclusive. He loved her for what she was, never asked for explanations, demanded nothing, and she felt a gust of resentment against Antoine. It was easy to talk of choice, of severing relations as if you could live for two years with a human being without becoming attached to him. She took Charles's hand and kept it. She felt an obligation to defend him, forgetting that this meant defending him against herself.

"I was very bored without you," said Charles. He smiled, tipped the porter, pointed out his bags to the chauffeur with his usual ease. She had not remembered how natural and simple things became with Charles. He opened the door of the car for her, walked to the other side, sat down by her, took her hands almost timidly, and said, "Home, please," joyfully, like a man really delighted to be back. She felt trapped.

"Why did you miss me? What can you still find to miss?"

Her voice was despairing, but Charles smiled, as though she were being coy.

"Everything, and you know it."

"I don't deserve it," she said.

"The idea of deserving, you know, in matters of sentiment . . . I've brought you a very pretty gift from New York."

"What is it?"

He refused to tell her, and they joked affectionately until they reached the flat. Pauline cried with relief on seeing them—to her any journey by plane was a mortal risk—and they unpacked Charles's bags together. He had brought her a mink coat, the same color as her light-gray eyes, soft and shining, and he laughed like a child when she tried it on. That afternoon, she telephoned Antoine, told him that she must see him, and that she had not had the courage to talk to Charles.

"I won't see you until you do," said Antoine simply.

His voice sounded very strange.

She did not see him for four days and, carried away by anger, did not suffer from his absence. She felt vindictive because he had hung up so abruptly when she telephoned: she detested all forms of rudeness. Anyway, she was almost sure that he would call her up again. They had been too closely united that last evening, had journeyed too far in love; they had become two celebrants of the same devotion, and this devotion now remained, in spite of the caprices of one or the other. Even if Antoine's attitude was hostile, her body knew his body, needed it, missed it. Their bodies were like two horses temporarily separated by their masters' estrangement, finally meeting again to gallop off together in a country sunny with pleasure. The contrary seemed impossible; she did not imagine that one could resist his desires; she had never seen a necessity or justification for opposing them. And in the fretful, bourgeois France of today, she could find no better principles than those instilled by hot and spirited young blood.

What she resented most in Antoine was that he had refused to allow her to explain. She would have told him that the plane was late, of her worry, and she would have proved her sincerity. Doubtless, she could have held to her decision and told Charles that evening, but she had tried so hard to put herself in a dramatic situation that it had seemed to be a mysterious omen. A certain kind of disloyalty makes for superstition. Meanwhile, Antoine did not telephone, and she was bored.

Summer arrived; people began holding open-air receptions, and Charles took her to an unpromising dinner at the Pré-Catelan. Diane and Antoine stood under a tree, the center of a very animated group, and Lucile heard Antoine's laugh before she saw him. She thought quickly:

So he laughs when I'm not there, but nevertheless a movement of joy swept her toward him. She held out her hand
with a smile, but he did not return her smile, bowed
quickly, and turned away. Then the fresh green park, the
brilliantly illuminated Pré-Catelan seemed dismal, and she
suddenly saw people's futility, their mental poverty, the
desperate tedium of this place, of her set, of her own life.
If there had not been Antoine, his yellow eyes, his room,
and the several hours of truth that she knew in his arms
three times a week, every detail of this confused and restless, though somewhat gay, world would have become the
hideous invention of a bad decorator. Claire Santré seemed
repulsively ugly, Johnny ridiculous, and Diane half dead.
She drew back.

"Lucile," called Diane in her imperious voice, "don't
run away like that. You're wearing a very pretty dress."

At present, Diane was very fond of showering sweet
nothings on Lucile. Thinking thus to prove her absolute
security. It made Johnny smile, and even more so Claire,
to whom he had finally confessed. Their little set knew all
about the affair, of course, and it was now, as Lucile and
Antoine stood side by side, pale, irresolute and tormented,
that they received the half-envious, half-sarcastic glances
reserved for new lovers. Lucile moved closer.

"The dress was new yesterday," she said mechanically,
"but I'm afraid it's a bit too chilly for this evening."

"It's easier to catch bronchitis in Coco Dourède's dress
than in yours," said Johnny. "I've never seen so little silk
cover so large a surface. What's more, she told me that it
could be washed like a handkerchief. It must take even less
time."

Lucile glanced at Coco Dourède, who was walking about
half naked under the garlands of electric lights. A deep,
delicious smell of earth rose from the Bois de Boulogne.

"You don't seem very cheerful, my dear," said Claire. Her eyes sparkled; her hand rested on Johnny's arm, and he too watched Lucile. Intrigued by her silence, Diane also looked at her. They're like dogs, thought Lucile, dogs so full of curiosity that they would tear me to pieces if they could. She smiled feebly.

"I feel really cold. I'm going to ask Charles for my coat."

"I'll go," said Johnny. "The young man in charge of the cloak room is superb."

He came back running. Lucile had not yet looked at Antoine, although she watched him in profile, as do certain birds.

"Why, it's a new coat!" cried Claire. "That pastel gray is divine; I've never seen you wear it."

"Charles brought it to me from New York," said Lucile.

At that moment her eyes met Antoine's, and what she read in them made her want to slap him. She turned brusquely and left the group.

"When I was young, mink coats made one look more joyful," said Claire.

But Diane frowned. Antoine, who stood by her, had assumed what she called his blind expression. Motionless, his face a blank.

"Get me a whisky," she said.

Not daring to ask him questions, she gave him orders.

Neither made a move toward the other during that evening. But around midnight, they found themselves at opposite ends of the table, alone, the others having gone to dance. He could not, without being rude, avoid joining her, and yet he did not want to be near her. He was crushed by the suffering he had endured for the last two days. He had pictured her in Charles's arms, embracing, saying the things that she had said to him. And above all, he had imagined her expression, an expression that was open and at the same time enclosed some passionately wild secret, an expression that he had won and that was now his sole ambition. He was mortally jealous. Walking around the table, he sat down by her.

She did not look at him, and, suddenly, he went to pieces and leaned forward. No, it was impossible, unbearable to be with this unconcerned stranger, this woman who had lain naked with him in the sun less than a week ago.

"Lucile," he asked, "what are you doing to us?"

"And you?" she asked. "You have a whim, and I'm to break with Charles in twenty-four hours. It was impossible."

She felt thoroughly desperate, thoroughly calm. Emptied.

"It's not a whim," he said jerkily. "I'm jealous and can't help it. I can't support lying any longer; it's killing me. I mean it. The idea that . . . that . . ." He paused, ran his hand over his face, and continued: "Tell me, since Charles has come back, have you . . ."

She turned violently toward him:

"Slept with him? Of course. He brought me a mink, didn't he?"

"You don't really believe what you're saying," said Antoine.

"No, but you believed it. I read it in your face a moment ago. I detest you for it."

A couple returned to the table, and Antoine rose quickly.

"Let's dance," he said. "I must talk to you."

"No," answered Lucile. "I've told you the truth, haven't I?"

"Perhaps . . . one can have unfortunate reflexes."

"But not vulgar reflexes," she replied, turning away.

She's putting me in the wrong, he thought; she's unfaithful, and she's putting me in the wrong. A wave of anger invaded him; he seized her wrist and drew her to him so roughly that several heads turned and looked at them.

"Come and dance."

She resisted, her eyes filled with tears of rage and pain. "I don't feel like dancing."

Antoine was his own prisoner, as incapable of letting her go as he was of dragging her away by force. At the same time he was fascinated by her tears; he thought quickly: I've never seen her cry. How I wish she would cry on my shoulder some night over an old childhood grief; I should like so much to comfort her.

"Antoine, let me go," she said in a low voice.

It was becoming grotesque. He was far stronger than Lucile, who had half risen from her chair, incapable of smiling foolishly, unconcernedly, as though the scene were a joke. People were staring at them. He was mad, mad and unkind; he frightened her, and she still found him attractive.

"It's what's called a hesitation waltz," said Charles, behind Antoine.

Antoine suddenly released Lucile, and turned. He would give the old fellow a big punch on the nose and leave all these people for ever. But next to Charles there was Diane, smiling, impeccable, slightly intrigued and, it seemed, distant.

"Are you trying to force Lucile to dance?" she asked.

"Yes," replied Antoine, staring at her. He was going to leave Diane that very evening; he realized it, and a feeling of calm came over him. And compassion, too. She counted for so little in this affair; she had never interested him.

"You're too old to play at being a teen-ager," she said.

She had already sat down. Charles, smiling, but with a grim face, leaned toward Lucile and asked her what had happened. Lucile returned his smile and, as she did not lack imagination, answered something or other. Everyone present had enough imagination to get out of a tight spot, to conceal, nourish, and sustain a little secret. Everyone but Antoine. He hesitated, made a curious half-turn, almost an entrechat, and strode away.

14

It was raining; she could hear the drops splash on the pavement. It must be one of the soft, sad summer rains, more like a gardener's desultory watering than the fury of the elements. Daylight was already stealing over the carpet; she was in bed and unable to sleep. Her heart thumped with excitement; she felt its agitation as the frenzied pulsations sent the blood to her body's extremities, coursing through the blue vein at her temple. She could not quiet her heart; she had supported it with a mixture of irony and despair for the past two hours. Since they had returned from the Pré-Catelan, soon after she had become aware of Antoine's disappearance, Diane's pallor, and the general rejoicing over the little scandal.

She was no longer angry; she even wondered what could have caused it. Antoine's expression during the mink-coat incident had seemed insulting. He seemed to have concluded that she was venal. But, in a certain way, wasn't she? She was supported by Charles, accepted and appreciated his presents—more because of his intention than their value, doubtless—but still, she accepted them. She could not deny it nor did she think of doing so, for it seemed so natural to be kept by a man who could afford it, and, moreover, a man she held in esteem. Antoine had grossly misinterpreted the situation: he thought that she stayed with Charles for mercenary reasons, that she had given him up for that; he believed her to be calculating, judged and no doubt despised her. She already knew that jealousy almost invariably leads to base arguments, actions, and judgments, but she could not bear that from Antoine, no matter how jealous he was. She had faith in him, believed that there existed a sort of family relationship, a moral complicity between them, and she felt as if she had received a low blow.

What could she say to him? Of course Charles brought me a mink coat, and I was delighted. Of course I have shared his bed since he came back, as we do from time to time. Of course that has nothing to do with what happens between you and me, because with us it's passion, and passion resembles nothing else. My body only has imagination, intelligence when it's with yours, and you should know that. But he did not understand that. It was a commonplace a thousand times quoted and a thousand times verified that men did not understand that kind of thing in a woman. She felt herself falling into the philosophy of a suffragette, and it vexed her. Do I mention his relations with Diane? I am not jealous; does that mean I am a monster? And if I am a monster, what can I do about it? Nothing. But if she did not change she would lose Antoine, and the idea made her shiver and turn over in her bed like a fish gasping on the grass. It was four o'clock in the morning.

Charles entered the bedroom. He sat down softly on the bed, his features drawn in the stark morning light; he really did look fifty, and the rather sporty foulard robe he wore did not help the impression. He laid his hand on Lucile's shoulder and remained motionless for a moment.

"So you aren't asleep either?"

She vaguely gestured no, tried to smile, to blame the Pré-Catelan's cooking. But she was too exhausted. She shut her eyes.

"Perhaps we should . . ." began Charles. He stopped, then continued in a firmer voice: "Could you leave? Alone or with me, for the south of France? You've always said that the sea cures everything."

It was useless to ask as to what cure he was alluding, and something about his questioning clearly pointed out the fact.

"The south of France," she repeated dreamily, "the south of France?"

And, her eyes still obstinately closed, she pictured the sea breaking on the beach, the color of the sand when the sun abandoned it at dusk. What she loved most and, doubtless, what she missed the most.

"I shall go with you as soon as you can leave," she said.

She opened her eyes to look at him, but he had turned his head. And she was astounded for a moment before feeling, with a sort of horror, the warmth of her own tears on her cheeks.

The Mediterranean coast was not very crowded early in May, and the only hotel, the only restaurant open belonged to them. After a week Charles began to have hope. Lucile spent hours in the sun, hours in the water, read a lot, talked to him about the books she read, ate broiled fish, played cards with the few couples on the beach, seemed happy. Content, at least. But she drank a great deal in the evening, and she had made love with him one night in such a violent way, almost aggressively, that he didn't recognize her. He did not know that her acts sprang from hope, the hope of seeing Antoine again. She became tanned to please him, ate to avoid looking starved, read books published by his

firm in order to discuss them with him; she drank to forget him and to induce sleep. She did not, of course, admit
to herself this hope; she lived like an animal resigned to
being cut in two. But sometimes, in a heedless moment,
when she ceased to cling desperately to the elements, when
she forgot to notice the warmth of the sun, the freshness
of the water, the softness of the sand, the memory of Antoine fell down on her like a stone, and she bore it with a
mixture of happiness and despair, lying with arms out-
stretched, crucified, not through the palms by nails, but
through the heart by the terrible lances of remembrance.
And it amazed her then to feel her heart turn over, emptied
by the shock, emptied and yet horribly cumbersome. What
did she care about the sun, the sea, and even the purely
physical well-being of her body, what did she care about
things that had once been sufficient to make her happy if
Antoine were not there to share them with her? She could
have gone swimming with him, clutched at his dripping
blond hair, made even blonder by the seawater, kissed him
between two waves, loved him on the dunes behind the
now deserted cabins, only a few feet away, sat motionless
with him in the evening to watch the swallows dip down
on the pink roofs. In the past, time had not only been something to kill; time had been a thing to coddle, cherish, to
stop from passing. When her thoughts became unbearable,
she would get up absently and go to the far end of the bar,
where Charles, in his deck chair, could not see her. She
drank, quickly, one, two cocktails under the barman's
vaguely sardonic eye. He took her for an alcoholic. But
what did it matter? She would no doubt end by becoming
one. She returned to the beach, lay down at Charles's feet,
and shut her eyes: the sun was white; she could no longer
distinguish the heat on her skin from that of the alcohol
that raced beneath it; she saw only a weak and hazy An-

toine, no longer strong enough to hurt her. It allowed her to breathe freely for a few hours, to recover a kind of animal, almost vegetative independence. Charles seemed happy, which was the important thing, and when she saw him walking toward her wearing flannel trousers, a carefully knotted scarf tucked inside his shirt collar, a dark-blue blazer, and moccasins, she pushed away the vision of Antoine in a shirt open to the waist, his narrow hips and long legs covered by old linen trousers, barefoot, hair straggling over his eyes. She had known many young men and, doubtless, it was not his youth that she loved. She had loved older men. She loved him for being his own age, just as she loved him for being blond, as she loved him for being puritanical, as she loved him for being sensual, as she loved him for having loved her, and as she loved him for, no doubt, no longer loving her. That was the way it was. Her love was there, fixed, like a wall between herself and the sunshine and the facility, even the taste, for living. And she was truly ashamed. Her only rule was happiness, and self-inflicted grief seemed inexcusable (which had assured the incomprehension, the almost perpetual reproaches, of other members of society all her life).

And now, I'm paying for it, she thought with disgust. Disgust made all the greater because she did not believe in debts, because the present moral and social taboos exasperated her, and because an eagerness, so often observed in others, to spoil life, made her shrink back a little, as she might have before some shameful disease. She had contracted this disease; she suffered, and suffered without finding any pleasure in hearing herself say so, which is surely one of the most disagreeable ways of suffering.

Charles was obliged to return to Paris. She accompanied him to the station, was affectionate, and promised to be good. He would return in six days, and he would call her up every evening. He did. But on the fifth day, late in the afternoon, when she absently picked up the telephone receiver, she heard Antoine's voice. She had not seen him for two weeks.

15

On leaving the Pré-Catelan, Antoine had walked through the Bois de Boulogne, talking to himself like a madman. Diane's chauffeur had run after him, offering his services; but to the man's amazement Antoine had given him a five-thousand-franc note, muttering, "Here, for all that time it's not much, but it's all I have with me." So intense was his desire to finish with Diane that he no doubt imagined that everyone was aware of it. He had walked up the Avenue de la Grande Armée, explained to an insistent prostitute that he knew quite enough women of her sort, and then turned to apologize. She had vanished, probably consoled, and he spent a fruitless half hour looking for her. Then he had entered a bar on the Champs-Elysées, tried to get drunk, scuffled vaguely with another drinker over an obscure political issue, although the true reason was that the poor fellow obstinately played the jukebox, and Antoine himself had wanted to play a record over and over, a tune that he had danced to, listened to, and hummed with Lucile. Ah, as long as I'm feeling miserable, I'm going to do it thoroughly, he thought. Having won his boxing match with the drunkard, he played his record eight times, to everyone's dismay, and, being without enough money, he was obliged to leave his identity card with the barman. He reached home at three in the morning, exhausted, and sobered by the fresh air. In short, he behaved like a young man. Sorrow sometimes gives a force, an enthusiasm, a vivacity equal to that given by exultation.

At his door was Diane, seated in the car. He recognized the Rolls-Royce from a distance and all but turned on his heel. Then, the thought of the chauffeur who must be waiting, haggard with sleepiness, for Madame's boy friend to be good enough to come home, made him decide. He opened the door of the car, and Diane stepped out, without a word. She had touched up her face in the car, and the dawn light, though it made her mouth look too red, gave her features, carefully indifferent, a new expression of youth, of bewilderment and error. And indeed, in her own eyes, she had made an error in pursuing her lover at dawn, as she had made an error two years ago in falling in love with him. Only this error, which until now had been like the background music to the film of her life, obstinate but discreet, now resounded like the relentless, cruel beating of a tom-tom. She saw herself leave the car, accept Antoine's helping hand; she saw herself make a final effort to maintain gracefully, for a few minutes more, the role of a beloved woman, before assuming the role, unknown and terrifying for her, of a woman scorned. And as she sent her chauffeur away, she smiled at him with a sort of strange intimacy, as though she knew that he was the last precious witness to her happiness.

"Am I disturbing you?" she asked.

Antoine shook his head. He opened the door of his room and stood aside to let her pass. This was the second time that she had come there. The first time, they had just met and it had amused Diane to spend their first night together in the room of this awkward and rather badly dressed young man. Afterward, she had offered him the large bed in the Rue Cambon flat, with all its pomp and luxury, because his room, after all, was really quite shabby and without comfort. And now she would have given all the world to sleep in that rickety bed and hang her clothes on the hideous chair next to it. Antoine shut the blinds, lighted the red lamp, and ran his hand over his face. He needed a shave and seemed to have grown thinner during the last few hours; in fact, he had the appearance of a tramp, the look that grief so often gives to a man. She no longer knew what she wanted to say to him. Ever since he had rushed away, she repeated the same sentence in her mind, over and over: He owes me an explanation. But, actually, what did he owe her, what can one owe to another? Sitting up very straight on the bed, she was tempted to lie down, to say: "Antoine, I simply wanted to see you, I was worried; now I'm drowsy, let's go to sleep." But Antoine was standing in the middle of the room; he waited, and everything in his attitude indicated that he wished to make clear, which meant to shatter, their situation, and in doing so, make her wretchedly unhappy.

"You left in quite a hurry," she said.

"I'm sorry."

They spoke like two actors; he felt it; he waited to have enough force and breath to say to her—like the trite but indispensable line in a play—"It's all over between us." He vaguely hoped for reproaches, that she would mention Lucile and that anger would give him the strength to be brutal. But she seemed gentle, resigned, almost frightened, and for a moment he thought with horror that he did not know her and that he had never tried to know her. Perhaps she cared for him in other ways, not just as a lover and a baffling human being. He had always imagined that the principal reasons for her attachment to him were her gratified sensuality and wounded pride (she had never been able to force him to unconditional surrender, as had been the case with her other males). And if there were something else? If Diane suddenly began to cry? But that was inconceivable. Diane's legend, that of being invulnerable and unrestrained, was too well known in Paris and he had heard it told repeatedly. For a second, they just missed knowing each other. Then she opened her handbag, took out a gold vanity case and touched up her face. It was the gesture of a panic-stricken woman, but he mistook it for a gesture of indifference. Anyway, Lucile doesn't love me, so no one can, he thought in conclusion, with a masochistic pessimism that came from his unhappiness, and he lighted a cigarette.

He threw the match in the hearth with an irritated and impatient movement that she attributed to boredom, and it rekindled her anger. She forgot Antoine, her passion for him; she thought only of herself, Diane Merbel, and the manner in which a man, her lover, had deserted her for no apparent reason in the midst of a party and in front of all her friends. She, in turn, took out a cigarette, her hand trembling, and he handed her a match. The smoke had an unpleasantly acrid taste; she had smoked too much and she suddenly realized that the confused, multifarious noise that had obsessed her for the last few minutes was from the birds in the street. Awake at dawn, crazy with joy, they joyously greeted the first rays of the sun. She looked at Antoine.

"May I ask why you ran away? Or perhaps it's none of my business."

"You may," replied Antoine. He looked squarely at her, and a slight grimace, unfamiliar, deformed his mouth. "I'm in love with Lucile . . . Lucile Saint-Léger," he added stupidly, as if there could possibly be an error.

Diane looked down. The top of her handbag was torn; she must change it. She stared at the tear, obstinately; it was the only thing that she could see. She tried to think clearly: Where could I have torn it? She waited, waited for her heart to start beating again, for daylight to burst into the room, for something to happen, no matter what, a telephone call, an atomic explosion, a shout from the street to drown her silent cry. But nothing happened. The birds went on chattering outside, and it was odious, this frenzy and disorder.

"Well, well," she said, "you might perhaps have warned me of this sooner."

"I didn't know," he answered. "I wasn't sure. I thought I was only jealous. But, you see, she doesn't love me; I know it now and I couldn't be unhappier . . ."

He could have gone on. In fact, this was the first time that he had ever mentioned Lucile to anyone. It gave him a kind of painful pleasure, and he forgot, unconscious as only a man can be, that he was talking to Diane. Anyway, she had remembered only the word "jealous."

"Why jealous? As you've so often explained, it's only possible to be jealous of what belongs to you. Have you been her lover?"

He did not reply. Anger surged up in Diane and freed her.

"You're jealous of Blassans-Lignières? Or has Lucile two or three other lovers? Anyway, if it can be of any comfort to you, my poor Antoine, you'll have a hard time supporting her alone."

"That's not the question," said Antoine dryly.

Suddenly, he hated Diane for judging Lucile, as he himself had done four hours earlier. He would not allow her to scorn Lucile. He had told the truth; she should go away now and leave him alone with the memory of Lucile at the Pré-Catelan, her eyes full of tears. Had she cried only because he had hurt her wrists, or because she loved him?

"Where did you have your meetings?" asked Diane's voice in the distance. "Here?"

95

"Yes. In the afternoon."

And he remembered Lucile's face when they made love, her body, her voice, all that he had lost through his own stupidity, his uncompromising attitude, and felt like kicking himself. There would be no more of Lucile's steps on the staircase, no more burning, marvelous afternoons, no more red and black, no more of anything. The face he turned to Diane was so sad and passionate that she drew back.

"I never thought you loved me," she said, "but I imagined that you had a certain regard for me. I'm afraid . . ."

He looked at her blindly, and his eyes showed her an immutable masculine world, a world where a man could not have regard for a mistress he did not love. He probably thought her a flattering conquest; he perhaps had a certain respect for her, but deep down in his heart he considered her as the lowest of prostitutes. For she had consented to live with him for two years without exacting his love or even his saying that he loved her, no more than she told him of her own love. And, too late, she saw in Antoine's yellow eyes an absolute, brutal, sentimental child, eager for words, scenes, and cries of love. Silence and elegance were not proof of love for the young. At the same time, she knew that if she rolled on the bed, pleaded with him, as she wanted to, he would be terrified and a little disgusted. He had become accustomed to the character she had personified for two years, to the profile she had obstinately turned to him for two years, and he would not recognize any other. Decidedly, she was paying dearly for her pride. But in this pride that made her sit up so straight on the bed at dawn, the pride so inseparable from the personage she had created that she almost ignored its existence, she now found her closest ally, the most intimate, the most precious. Just as a born horseman suddenly discovers that it is his thirty years of riding that have permitted him to pass unharmed under a bus. Diane thought with astonishment of her pride, this forgotten, or at least poorly used inheritance, that now spared her the worst: the worst would be to behave, Antoine no longer loving her, in such a manner as to be unbearable in her own eyes.

"Why tell me all this now?" she asked quietly. "Things could have gone on as they were for a long time. I had only the vaguest suspicion, or rather, I didn't believe it true any longer."

And he realized with bewilderment that it was true; he could have lied to Diane all night, comforting and convincing her, if he had been sure of meeting Lucile the next day, or that she loved him. Happiness permits everything and, for a second, he understood Lucile, her facility, her capacity for dissimulation that he had so harshly criticized during the last weeks. It was too late, too late. He had mortally wounded her; she would have nothing more to do with him. But what was this other woman doing in his room? Diane divined his thoughts, and attacked blindly:

"And your dear Sarah? What happens to her in all of this?" she asked gently. "Is she finally dead, for good and all?"

He did not answer. He looked at her with fury now, but she preferred that to the friendly, distant expression he had shown her several moments before. She drifted straight toward the worst, toward the lack of understanding, cruelty, the unpardonable, and she felt relieved.

"I think you had better leave now," he said at last. "I shouldn't like us to part on bad terms. You have always been so good to me."

"I've never been good to anyone," said Diane, as she rose. "Under certain circumstances, I thought you rather agreeable, that's all."

Standing very straight, she looked him in the face. He could not know that a passing memory, a regretful expression would have sufficed for her to fall weeping into his arms. But he had no regrets, and she simply held out her hand and watched Antoine mechanically bow over it; the expression of uncontrolled grief that she had shown as she looked for this last time at Antoine's bent, blond nape had disappeared when he raised his head. She murmured, "Good-bye," brushed through the doorway, and started down the stairs. Antoine's flat was on the fourth floor, but it was only when she reached the first-floor landing that she paused, pressing close to the damp, dirty wall the celebrated face, the beautiful hands that were now so useless.

16

Antoine spent fifteen days alone. He took long walks, spoke to no one, and was not even surprised, when he met an acquaintance, a friend of Diane's, at being ignored. He knew the rules of the game: Diane had introduced him into a set that was not his, and he was automatically rejected from it when he left her. That was the rule, and Claire's hasty graciousness when she met him by chance one evening was the most he could expect. She informed him, however, that Charles and Lucile were at Saint-Tropez, without showing the least surprise that Antoine did not know it. It seemed obvious that by giving up one woman, he had also lost the other. The idea amused him faintly, although this was a time when he felt less and less inclined to laugh. One of Apollinaire's sentences obsessed him: "I wander about my lovely Paris without having the heart to die there. The herds of bellowing buses . . ." He could not recall what followed, and did not, for that matter, try to remember. It was true that Paris was breathtakingly beautiful, blue, blond, languid; it was true that he had no more the heart to die there than to live there. All was for the best. Lucile was on the shores of the Mediterranean that she had told him she loved; she must be happy once again, since she was made for that, and perhaps she was deceiving Charles with one of the handsome local youths. Diane was seen about with a young Cuban diplomat; he had seen a charming photograph of the couple in a newspaper, taken at a first-night performance of the ballet. As for himself, he had stopped drinking; he read, and sometimes at night, in bed, he twisted with fury thinking of Lucile. This was evidently his fate. He no longer hoped; his memory could give him no reason for that. His only memory was of Lucile's pleasure, of his own, a memory that ravaged without reassuring him, for one can never be entirely sure of the intensity of another's pleasure—or if such intensity could not be reached or even surpassed with a stranger. Although he knew that no one but Lucile could give him as much sensual pleasure, he could not imagine that this held true for her. At times, he remembered her hunted expression that day when he had arrived so late; he recalled that she had said, "I love you for keeps, you know." He thought that he had missed a chance that day; he should have devoted more time to Lucile's feelings and less to her body, and also, that if he had doubtless possessed her physically, he had totally failed to possess her spirit. Of course, they laughed together, and it was the laughter of love, but that was not enough. To understand, he had only to recall the strange melancholy that had overcome him, in the middle of his anger, on discovering the tears in Lucile's eyes at the Pré-Catelan. For a man and a woman truly to love, it is not enough that they offer each other pleasure, make each other laugh; they must also make each other suffer. She could well argue the contrary. But she would no longer argue anything with him; she had gone. He broke off the dialogue, the explanation he mentally had with her twenty times a day, jumped up suddenly from his chair or suddenly stopped walking. This went on endlessly.

On the fifteenth day, he met Johnny, on holiday and wandering about the Flore, who seemed delighted to see him again. They took a table, had a whisky together, and Antoine was amused by Johnny's priggish manner when he returned the greetings of his friends. Johnny knew himself to be rather goodlooking, just as he knew himself to be blond, but without further interest.

"So how is Lucile?" asked Johnny, at one moment.

"I really don't know."

Johnny began to laugh.

"I knew it. You were right to end it. She's charming but dangerous. She'll probably end in being an alcoholic under Charles's tender care."

"What makes you think so?" Antoine watched over his voice, its carefully calculated indifference.

"She's begun. One of my friends saw her staggering about the beach. But that shouldn't surprise you."

Before Antoine's expression, he started to laugh.

"Come now, you know that she was madly in love with you; it could be seen from twenty feet, even if one didn't already know. What's the matter with you?"

Antoine laughed; he could not stop laughing, he was mad with happiness, mad with shame. He was stupid, he had been too stupid. Of course she loved him, of course she thought of him. How could he have believed that she did not love him, after having been so happy with him for two months? How could he have been so pessimistic, so selfish, so thoughtless? She loved him, she missed him, and she drank on the sly because of it. Maybe she even believed he had forgotten her, when he had done nothing but think of her these last fifteen days; perhaps she was unhappy because of his gross stupidity. He would go to her at once, explain everything, do anything she wanted; but he would take her in his arms, beg her pardon, they would embrace for hours. Where was Saint-Tropez?

He had got up from his chair.

"Now then," said Johnny, "keep calm. You look like a raving maniac, my dear friend."

"Sorry," said Antoine, "I must make a telephone call."

He ran all the way to his flat, quarreled with a telephone operator who was slow in explaining how the dial system worked in the Var, tried three hotels, and was informed by the fourth that Mademoiselle Saint-Léger was on the beach, but would be coming in soon. He placed a person-to-person call and settled down on the bed, his hand on the receiver, like Lancelot of the Lake holding the hilt of his sword, ready to wait two hours, six hours, his whole life—happier, he thought, than he had ever been.

At four o'clock the telephone rang, and he picked up the receiver.

"Lucile? It's Antoine."

"Antoine," she repeated, as though she were dreaming.

"I must . . . I should like to see you. May I come to Saint-Tropez?"

"Yes," she answered. "When?"

And although she spoke calmly, he recognized in her terse reply the fall and retreat of the horrible, the cruel thing that had twisted, shaken, maltreated them both during fifteen days. He saw his own hand lying on the bed; he was surprised to see that it did not tremble.

"There must be a plane," he said. "I'm leaving at once. Will you meet me at Nice?"

"Yes," she said. She hesitated, then added, "Are you at home?"

He repeated her name three times into the telephone: "Lucile, Lucile, Lucile . . ." before answering affirmatively.

"Hurry," she said, and hung up.

His only thoughts at the moment were that perhaps she was with Charles and that he could not afford to take a plane. But they were casual thoughts. He felt capable of robbing his neighbor or killing Charles or piloting a Boeing. And, in fact, at seven thirty, he could have taken the hostess's advice and, to the left of the plane, admired the city of Lyons if he had wanted to do so.

After the call, Lucile closed her book, took a sweater out of the closet, the keys of the car that Charles had rented and went downstairs. She caught a glimpse of herself in a mirror that defaced the hotel lobby and she gave herself a furtive, undecided smile, the kind one shows to a very sick person, condemned by the doctors, and who suddenly leaves the hospital, apparently cured. She must drive very carefully; the road was in bad condition and full of curves. An imprudent dog, a speed demon, a material accident must not come between her and Antoine, and she thought practically only of that, as if drugged, lost to herself until she reached the airport. There was an arrival from Paris at six o'clock; and though there was no chance that he would be there, she waited at the exit. The next plane was at eight o'clock, and she bought a detective novel, installed herself at the bar, upstairs, and vainly tried to understand what was happening to a private detective, usually fascinating, who was now incapable of holding her interest. She knew the expression "an overpowering happiness" but she had never verified its truth, and she was surprised to feel as if she had been through the mill, broken, exhausted to such a point that she wondered if she would not faint or fall asleep in her chair before eight o'clock. She called the waiter and informed him that she was expecting someone on the eight o'clock plane, which seemed, however, of only mediocre interest to the man. But at least if anything happened to her, he could let Antoine know. How she did not know, but every precaution must be taken to protect the new, bewildered, frail, happy person that she had at last become. She went so far as to change tables so that she could see the bar's huge clock, as the loudspeakers were impossible to understand. After she had conscientiously looked at all the printing on the pages of her book, it was only seven o'clock, a tearful woman embraced a wounded but triumphant detective in a Miami hospital, and her own heart ached.

An hour, two months, thirty years went by before Antoine appeared at the far end of the hall, the first passenger, for he had no luggage. And as he took the few steps that separated them, she thought only that he looked thin, very pale, badly dressed, that she scarcely knew him; the same detached conscience admitted too that she loved him. He came up to her awkwardly; they shook hands without looking at each other much, and hesitated for a moment before moving toward the exit. He murmured that she was tanned; she hoped, aloud, that he had had a pleasant trip. After which, they got into the car; she showed Antoine where the starter was, and they drove off. It was a warm evening; the odor of the sea blended with the smell of the automobile, and the airport's palm trees stirred gently in

103

the wind. They drove for a few miles without talking or even knowing where they were going; then Antoine stopped the car and took her in his arms. He did not kiss her, but simply held her close, his cheek against hers, and she could have wept with relief. When he did speak, it was very low, gently, like a child.

"Where is Charles?" he asked. "He must be told."

"Yes," she said. "He is in Paris."

"We'll take the train tonight. There is a night train, isn't there? We can take it at Cannes."

She agreed tacitly and moved away a little to look at him, to see his eyes, at last, and the shape of his mouth. He leaned forward to kiss her. There was one berth left on the train at Cannes. All night long there were the shrieks of the train, the flashes of light on their united faces, and occasionally, when they stopped at a station, the loud metallic sound of the railroad hand who, with his iron rod, watched over the safety of the wheels, their progress toward Paris, their destiny. It seemed to them that the train's speed doubled with their pleasure, that it had gone mad, and that it was themselves who pushed this feverish motion in the sleeping countryside.

"I knew it," said Charles.

He turned his back and leaned his forehead against the windowpane. She was sitting on her bed, exhausted. Her ears still echoed with the train's roar. When they had reached the Gare de Lyon early that morning, it was raining. Then she had telephoned Charles from his flat, their flat, and she had waited for him there. He had come very quickly, and she told him immediately that she was in love with Antoine and that she must leave him. And now, as he pretended to look out of the window, she was surprised that his neck should remain so straight and that the fact did not stir her, whereas Antoine's neck and his stiff tangled hair moved her so much. It seemed impossible to remember that some men had ever been children.

"I imagined that it would be of no importance," said Charles. "You see, I hoped—" He stopped short and turned to her: "You must understand that I love you. Don't think that I shall be resigned to this or forget you or replace you. I'm no longer young enough for substitutions." He smiled faintly. "You will come back to me, Lucile. I love you for yourself. Antoine loves you for what you are together. He wants to be happy with you; that's the way it is at his age. I want you to be happy independently of me. All I have to do is to wait."

She made a protesting gesture, but he quickly raised his hand.

"What's more, he will blame you, or already has, for being what you are: an easygoing, rather cowardly epicure. He will naturally resent what he will call your faults or weaknesses. He does not yet understand that what makes a woman's strength, reason why men love her, even if that reason conceals the worst. He will learn that with you. He will learn that you are gay, funny, and kind because you have all these faults. But it will be too late. At least, so I think. And you will come back to me. Because you know that I know."

He gave a light laugh.

"I haven't accustomed you to such long speeches, have I? Now tell him, from me, that if he hurts you, that if, in a month or in three years, he doesn't give you back to me, whole and happy as you are now, I shall break every bone in his body."

He spoke almost angrily, and she looked at him, stunned.

105

She did not know that he was capable of giving such an impression of strength, almost of violence.

"I'm not trying to persuade you to stay; it would be useless, wouldn't it? But remember this well: I'm waiting for you. No matter when. And no matter what you want of me, no matter why, it will be yours. Are you leaving right away?"

She nodded.

"You are taking everything of yours with you." And even as she shook her head; definite: "No, I couldn't bear to see your coats in the wardrobe or your car in the garage. Your absence may be long, after all. . . ."

Inert, she looked at him. She knew it would be like this: horrible, and that he would be like this: perfect. Everything had taken place just as she had long imagined, and with the despair she felt at his suffering was mingled a pride in having been loved by him. She couldn't leave him like this, in this immense flat, all alone. She got up.

"Charles," she said. "I . . ."

"No," he replied. "You've waited long enough. Be on your way now."

He stood still for a moment, staring at her so intently that his expression was almost dreamy. Then he bent quickly, his lips touched her hair, and he turned away.

"You must go now. I'll send your bags to the Rue de Poitiers later."

She was not surprised that he knew Antoine's address. She despised herself so much that she could see nothing but Charles's slight stoop, his gray hair, feeling that she had caused them. She whispered: "Charles . . ." not knowing whether she wanted to say "thank you" or "forgive me" or some other tactless remark, for he made a feverish, broken gesture, without turning, as much as to signify that he could not support much more, and she backed out of the

106

room. On the staircase, she realized that she was crying, and went to the kitchen, where she collapsed, sobbing, on the shoulder of Pauline, who assured her that men were all tedious and not worth weeping over. Antoine was waiting for her outside, in a café, in the sun.

Part Two

Summer

17

She felt that she was the victim of a strange, wonderful disease that she knew to be happiness, although she hesitated to call it so. In a way, she found it fantastic that two intelligent, nervous, and critical human beings should arrive at this degree of intimate unity, at this point exhausted of aspirations, that all they could say was "I love you" with a sort of sob in their voice, for there was nothing to add. She knew that there was nothing else to add, nothing more to be hoped for, that this was what is called completeness, but she asked herself what she would do later to survive the memory of this completeness. She was happy; she was afraid.

They told each other everything: their childhood, their past, and always, always they returned to the last few months, recounting endlessly, like all lovers, their first meetings, the tiniest details of their affair. They wondered with amazement (real and a little foolish) but normal, how they could have doubted their true feelings for so long. But if they reveled in their troubled and turbulent past together, they did not dream of a mutual future that was to be peaceful and lasting. Lucile, even more than Antoine, was afraid of projects, of the simple life. Meanwhile, they watched, fascinated, the present unfold, the day break to find them together in the same bed, never wearying of each other, the sky darken at twilight to find them walking about a warm, tender, incomparable Paris. And, at certain moments, they were so happy that it seemed to them as though they were no longer in love.

It was enough for Antoine to be an hour late that Lucile,

who had watched him leave with a calm, almost an indifference, so total that she began to doubt to have been as she had been at Saint-Tropez: that sick, ravaged, voiceless animal—for Lucile to begin to shake with fear, to imagine Antoine's body lying under a bus, and in her mind to define his presence as happiness, since his absence meant despair. And it was enough that Lucile smile at another man for Antoine (the constant, physical possession of her body—even if he did not tire of it—reassured him completely) to grow pale, to change happiness into something fragile, temporary and forever insecure. Even in their most tender moments, there was something disquieting and violent between them. And if at times they suffered from this uneasiness, they also knew, strangely, that if it disappeared in either of them, their love would vanish with it. In fact, the foundation of their relationship had been determined by two almost equal sentimental shocks: for her, Antoine's lateness, that unforgettable afternoon, and for him, Lucile's refusal to leave with him the day of Charles's return from America. And Lucile—whose modesty was as marked as her pride, as with most carefree people—thought hazily that someday Antoine would not come back, just as Antoine thought in the same way that Lucile would be unfaithful to him some evening. These two wounds that happiness should have healed, they kept open, almost deliberately, just as a man who has survived a serious accident takes pleasure, after six months of suffering, in scratching open the last sore, the better to enjoy the perfect condition of the rest of his body. Each of them had need of a thorn in their flesh: Antoine because of a profound need, Lucile, because this shared happiness was too unfamiliar.

Antoine woke early in the morning, and his body recognized, before his mind, Lucile's presence in the bed, wanted it, even before he opened his eyes. Sleepily, smiling, he edged closer to her, torn from his last dreams by a little moan of Lucile's or the clutch of her hand on his body. He slept deeply, heavily, like some men and most children, and nothing pleased him more than these slow, voluptuous awakenings. As for Lucile, her first sensation in the morning was one of pleasure, and she recovered consciousness surprised, delighted, and vaguely annoyed by a semi-rape that deprived her of her usual awakening: opening, then shutting her eyes, refusing or accepting to face another day, the tender, confused little battle she fought against herself. Sometimes, she tried to cheat, to awaken before he did, but Antoine never slept more than six hours and always forestalled her. He laughed at her furious expression; he delighted in tearing her from the darkness of sleep to plunge her so quickly into the darkness of love; he liked most of all the moment when she opened her eyes, bewildered, undecided, and finally understanding, then shutting them at once, as though obliged, as she slipped her arms around his neck.

Lucile's suitcases were piled on top of the wardrobe, and only two or three dresses, Antoine's favorites, hung side by side with his two suits. On the other hand, the bathroom clearly showed a woman's presence by the numbers of small jars, most of them unused, that were displayed. As he shaved, Antoine indulged in lengthy commentaries about the use of herb masks in eliminating wrinkles, and other facetious remarks. Lucile retorted that he would be glad enough someday to have it available, that he was aging by the minute, and that he was, in fact, quite ugly. He kissed her. She laughed. It was particularly fine that summer in Paris.

He left for his work at nine thirty, and she stayed quietly in the room, longing for a cup of tea, but incapable of making the effort to go to the corner café. She picked up one of the hundred books stacked in every corner of the room, and read. The church clock that had made her suffer so one afternoon struck each half hour and, at present, she loved its booming sound. At times, when she heard it, she put down her book and smiled into space, as at a recaptured childhood. At eleven or eleven thirty Antoine would call up, his voice often casual, but sometimes with the quick, decided tone of a man overloaded with work. In that case, Lucile answered gravely, though laughing inwardly, for she knew him to be lazy and a dreamer, but she had reached that stage in love where one feels as much tenderness for the other's nonsense as for his truths, or even, on the contrary, his part truths, because they are recognized as such, and appear as a sign of ultimate confidence. At noon they met at the swimming pool at the Concorde and ate a sandwich together in the sun. Then he went back to work, unless the sun, the contact of their slightly tanned, naked bodies, their conversation took them to his room, their room, and he would return late to his office. Afterward, Lucile began her long, idle walk through Paris; she met friends or vague acquaintances, drank tomato juice in sidewalk cafés. And everybody talked to her because she looked happy. In the evening, there were movies, the hot roads around Paris, the half-empty cabarets where she taught him to dance, all the unknown, tranquil faces of the city in summer; and all the words they wanted to speak and all the things they wanted to do.

At the end of July, by chance they ran into Johnny at the Flore, who had just returned from an exhausting weekend at Monte Carlo, accompanied by a curly-haired young man named Bruno. Johnny congratulated them for looking so content and asked why they did not get married. They laughed heartily and pointed out to him that they were not the sort to worry about the future and that the idea itself was ridiculous. Johnny agreed, and laughed with them. But after they were gone he murmured, "It's a pity," in a tone that puzzled Bruno. In answer to his questions, Johnny offered only a strange, melancholy look that the boy did not recognize, and said, "You wouldn't understand, but it was too late," an answer that amply satisfied Bruno, whose role it was, in fact, never to understand anything.

August came, and Antoine had a month's holiday. But he was out of money and, consequently, remained at home with Lucile.

It suddenly turned very hot in Paris that August; the air was oppressive and sultry, and brief, violent showers left the streets exhausted but fresh, like convalescents or young mothers after childbirth. Lucile spent most of the three weeks in a dressing gown, on her bed. Her summer wardrobe consisted of bathing suits or cotton slacks designed for the balmy days at Monte-Carlo or Capri where she usually went with Blassans-Lignières, and there was no question of adding to it. She read extensively, smoked, went out to buy tomatoes for lunch, made love with Antoine, discussed books with him, and went to sleep. The storms, of which she had such fear, threw her into his arms and he would comfort her, giving long scientific explanations and somber accounts of cumulus formations that she only half believed, and he called her "my little pagan," emotion in his voice. But he could not manage to make her share his emotion until the last clap of thunder had long since disappeared. At times he glanced at her, furtively, inquiringly. Lucile's laziness, her enormous capacity for idleness, never looking ahead, her faculty for happiness—to pass days so empty, so lifeless and monotonous—at times seemed to him fantastic, almost monstrous. He was sure that she loved him, could no more be bored with him than he with her, but he felt that this mode of life was what came closest to her real nature, while he knew that it was only passion that caused him to support this perpetual vacuity. It seemed as though he had come across a mysterious animal, an unknown plant, a mandrake. Then he would turn to her, slip between the sheets, never tiring of their pleasure, their blended perspiration, their exhaustion, and he proved to himself, in the most precise manner, that she was only a woman. They had gradually acquired an exact knowledge of their bodies, had all but made a sort of science of it, a fallible science, as it was based on a concern for the pleasure of the other, and it often disappeared, disarmed and power-less, before one's own pleasure. Such moments made it seem impossible that they had not known each other for thirty years. And a day could not die when they were not obliged to admit to themselves, again and again, that nothing else was true, nothing had value except the mo-ment that they were living then.

So August went by like a dream. The night before the first of September, toward midnight, they lay side by side, and Antoine's alarm clock, useless for a month, resumed its frantic march. It would ring at eight o'clock. Antoine lay on his back, motionless, and his hand, holding a cigarette, was hanging outside the bed. The rain had begun to fall in the street, slowly, softly, and he guessed that it was warm; he even imagined that it was salty like the tears dropping quietly on his cheek from Lucile's open eyes. He had no need to ask the reason for these falling drops, neither of Lucile nor the clouds. He knew that summer was over and that it had been the finest summer of their lives.

Part Three

Autumn

I saw that all beings are fated to be happy. Action is not life, but the means of squandering vigor, a nervous irritation.

ARTHUR RIMBAUD

18

Lucile impatiently awaited the bus at the Place de l'Alma. It was a particularly cold and rainy November, and the little bus shelter was crowded with shivering, sullen, almost aggressive people. She had preferred to wait outside, her wet hair sticking to her face. What was more, she had forgotten to take a waiting-number when she arrived. And there was, of course, a woman who snickered nastily when Lucile remembered it, six minutes later. At that moment, she bitterly regretted her car, the sound of rain pattering on its hood, the uncertain curves that she took on the wet cobblestones. The only real charm of money, she thought, was that it permitted one to avoid all this: the exasperation, the other people. She had been to the Palais de Chaillot film library, where Antoine, annoyed by her indolence, had, in an almost imperious tone, advised her to see one of Pabst's masterpieces. The film really was a masterpiece, but she had been obliged to stand in line for a half hour with a band of boisterous, impudent students, and she asked herself why she had not stayed quietly at home and finished the book by Simenon that so fascinated her. It was now six thirty; she would arrive later than Antoine, and perhaps this would cure him of a deplorable mania he had developed: involving Lucile in outside activities. He said that it was not normal, not healthy, that, after having led a busy social life for three years, with what he termed relationships with others, she now shut herself up in a room, with nothing to do. She could not tell him that she was beginning to discover that a city, even Paris, became terrifying, with only some bus tickets and two hundred francs in your pocket when you were accustomed to living otherwise. It would have humiliated him almost as much as it did her. She recalled having lived like that at twenty, and she did not care for the idea of beginning again at thirty. A bus arrived; the first numbers, far from hers, were called, and the poor wretches who did not get on the bus returned to their glass rabbit hutch. A kind of animal despair overcame Lucile. In half an hour, with a little luck, she would catch the bus that took her within three hundred yards of Antoine's room, three hundred yards that she would walk in the rain so that she would arrive tired, ugly, disheveled, to join a man as weary as she was. And if he asked enthusiastically what she thought of Pabst, she would be tempted to tell him about the crowd, the buses, the infernal regime to which workers are subjected, and he would be disappointed. A bus went by without stopping. Suddenly, she decided to walk home. An old lady walked up to the machine that dispensed the tickets. Lucile impulsively offered her own:

"Here, take mine, I'm walking home."

The woman gave her an inquiring, almost hostile glance. Perhaps she thought that Lucile acted out of charity, because she was old, or Heaven knows what. People were becoming distrustful. They were so full of worries, problems, stupid television and hysterical newspapers, that they no longer had a notion of largess.

Lucile was almost apologetic: "I live quite near; I'm already late and the rain has let up a bit, hasn't it?"

The "hasn't it?" was almost a plea, she thought, as she glanced insincerely at the sky, for it was raining as hard as ever. At the same time, she thought: What do I care if the woman disapproves of me? If she doesn't want the ticket, she can throw it away. I really don't mind if she waits another half hour. She felt totally helpless: What came over me? I should have done like everyone else: thrown it away. What is this mania to want to please, to establish affectionate relations with the Place de l'Alma, at six thirty in the evening, in front of a bus? To want everyone to love me? Affectionate relations, great sentimental outbursts with strangers take place between two whiskies, at people's homes if they can afford it, or in a secluded bar, or during a revolution. At the same time, she desperately wanted to prove herself wrong. The woman stretched out her hand and took the ticket.

"That's very kind of you," she said, smiling.

Lucile returned her smile and moved away. She would follow the quay to the Concorde, cross the river, and walk down the Rue de Lille. She suddenly remembered having taken the same walk one evening, the first evening, when she had met Antoine. But spring had just begun then, the young man was a stranger, and they had wandered of their own free will in the warm, solitary night, ignoring the taxis for reasons other than those that prevented her from hailing one now. I really must stop grumbling, she thought. What were they doing tonight? They were supposed to dine with Lucas Solder, a friend of Antoine's. Solder was a fervent and garrulous journalist with a marked taste for abstract ideas. He amused Antoine and would have amused Lucile if his wife, who had not kept up with her husband, had not always tried to engage Lucile in conversations that ranged from the latest bargain sales to female disorders. Moreover, Nicole, who liked to do things herself, concocted economical, uneatable dinners. "I should have been happy to dine at the Relais-Plaza," muttered Lucile as she walked on. "I would have had a frozen daiquiri with the barman, and ordered a hamburger and a salad. Instead of a thick soup, the revolting stew, dried cheese and the three sorts of fruit that are waiting for me. You'd think only the rich had a right to light meals. . . ." She lulled herself for a moment with this dream, the half-empty Plaza bar, the affable waiters, and she, sitting alone at a table, idly reading a newspaper and watching American women in mink coats as they went by. A little sick at heart, she realized that the dream did not include Antoine, that she had imagined herself without him. It had been a long time since she had had a meal alone, it was true, but she felt guilty. She ran down the Rue de Lille and up the stairs. Antoine lay on the bed, reading *Le Monde*—she apparently was fated to live with men who read *Le Monde*. He sat up, and she threw herself into his arms. He was warm, smelled of cigarette smoke, and looked immense stretched out like that on the bed; she never tired of his bony body, the light eyes, the strong hands that brushed aside her dripping hair. He muttered something about crazy women who wandered about in the rain.

"Well," he asked at last, "what about the film?"

"It was magnificent," she said.

"Admit that I was right in sending you to see it."

"Yes, I admit it," she answered.

She was standing in the bathroom, admitting still, a towel in her right hand, and she saw suddenly, in the mirror, a mysterious little smile. She was disconcerted for an instant, then slowly passed the towel over the glass, as though wiping away an accomplice who should not have been there.

19

She waited for Antoine in the small bar on the Rue de Lille where they habitually met about six thirty in the evening. She discussed racing with a waiter named Etienne, a rather good-looking, very talkative man, whom Antoine suspected of harboring a sentimental weakness for Lucile. She had sometimes taken his advice about horses, and the results were always disastrous, and Antoine, when he arrived, glanced at them suspiciously, not from jealousy but from fear of a material calamity. Lucile was in very good spirits that day. They had slept late after spending the night in making triumphant, complicated plans that she could no longer remember very clearly, but which sent them rapidly to the seashore, to Africa, or to an ideal country house near Paris. Meanwhile, Etienne, his eyes sparkling, talked to her of a certain Ambroisie II, quoted at ten-to-one, who was a sure thing at Saint-Cloud the next day. And the solitary, thousand-franc note that slept in Lucile's pocket would no doubt have changed hands if Antoine had not arrived looking excited. He kissed Lucile, sat down, and ordered two whiskies, which, considering that it was the twenty-sixth of the month, was a sign of celebration.

"What's happened?" asked Lucile.

"I talked to Sirer," said Antoine, and, faced with Lucile's perplexed expression, "you know, the editor of *Le Réveil*. He has a job for you, in the morgue."

"The morgue?"

"Yes, it's interesting enough, not too much work and

he'll give you a hundred thousand francs a month as a start."

She looked at him, aghast. Now she remembered what they had talked about the night before. They had agreed that Lucile's life was not the life for her, that she should do something. She had enthusiastically welcomed the idea of working, she had even developed a poetical picture of herself working for a newspaper, climbing the ladder, rung by rung, to become one of the brilliant women journalists of whom they talked so much in Paris; of course, she would have plenty of work and many worries, but she felt that she had enough courage, humor, and ambition to reach the top. They would rent a magnificent flat, at the paper's expense, as they would be forced to entertain a great deal, but every year they could escape and go boating, for at least a month, on the Mediterranean. She had expanded this theory with fervor before Antoine, who was at first skeptical, but he gradually became interested, for nothing could be more convincing than Lucile with a project, especially when it was a project so crazy, so contrary to her personality as this one. But what could she have drunk or read last night to launch her on such a scheme? She had no more ambition than she had tenacity, no more desire for a career than to commit suicide.

"It's very good pay for that type of paper, you know," said Antoine.

He seemed delighted with himself. She looked at him with affection: he was still under the influence of their nocturnal conversation; he must have thought about it all day, moved heaven and earth. It was extremely difficult to find that sort of job, so numerous were the housewives who, at the verge of nervous breakdowns caused by idleness, would have paid to scrub floors provided it was in a publishing house, fashion salon, or a newspaper office. And now, there was that crazy Sirer actually ready to pay her. She, who liked nothing but idleness. Life was stupid. She tried to smile at Antoine.

"You don't seem enchanted," he said.

"It seems too good to be true," she replied gloomily.

He threw her an amused glance. He knew very well that she regretted her nocturnal decisions; he also knew that she did not dare to tell him so. But he truly thought that she could not avoid boredom living as she did, that she would become weary of life and of him. In a whisper, he also told himself that a hundred thousand francs, added to his own salary, would offer Lucile an easier life. With a man's optimism, he imagined Lucile gaily buying two little dresses each month. Naturally, they would not be original models, but they would suit her perfectly because she had such a good figure. She would take taxis, see her friends, take a little interest in politics, the world in general, in others at last. He would doubtless be sorry not to find her waiting when he came home, like an animal snuggled into its burrow, this woman who subsisted only on books and love, but nevertheless he would feel vaguely reassured. For there was something about this static life, the veracity of the present, the contempt for the future that frightened, even vaguely vexed him, as if she were only an element of decoration, a studio setting, that one burns, inexorably, when the film is finished.

"When do I begin?" asked Lucile.

She was really smiling now. She could, after all, try. She had worked before, in her younger days. She would probably be a little bored, but she would hide that from Antoine.

"The first of December. In five or six days. Are you pleased?"

She threw him a suspicious glance. Could he really believe that she was pleased? She had already noted streaks of sadism in him. But he looked innocent, convinced. She nodded gravely:

"I'm very pleased. You're right, it couldn't have lasted."

He leaned across the table and kissed her so tenderly, so impulsively, that she knew he understood her. Her cheek against his, she smiled, and they made fun of her, together, indulgently. And, of course, she was relieved that he understood, because she did not like him to mislead himself concerning her, but at the same time she kept a slight resentment because she had pretended.

At home that evening, Antoine, pencil in hand, indulged in optimistic financial calculations. He would, of course, take care of the rent, the telephone bill, the tiresome small expenses. Lucile's hundred thousand francs would pay for her dresses, carfare, and lunches—there was a very good cafeteria, very gay, at the Réveil, where he could have lunch with her. . . . Lucile, seated on the bed, listened with stupefaction to these figures. She wanted to tell him that a dress from Dior cost three hundred thousand francs, that she hated the bus—even if it was direct—and that the very word cafeteria made her want to run away. She felt snobbish, exasperatingly and definitively snobbish. But when he had stopped walking up and down, and had turned to her with an undecided smile, as though he did not believe it himself, she could not help smiling back. He was like a child: he kept daily accounts as all children do; he established budgets like a state minister; he played with numbers as men love to do. What did it matter, after all, if her own life had to conform to these chimerical equations, as long as it was Antoine who expressed them?

20

It seemed that she had been there for years, but it had only been fifteen days since she had entered the office at Le Réveil. It was a large, gray room, crowded with desks, cupboards, and filing cabinets, and the only window looked out on a small street in the market district. She worked with a young woman called Marianne; three months pregnant, very likable, very efficient, who spoke with the same moving vigilance of the future of the newspaper and the expected child. She referred to them both in the masculine gender, certain that the baby would be a boy, and it sometimes happened that Lucile, when Marianne proffered an optimistic remark, such as, "They won't stop talking about him," or, "He'll go far," wondered for a moment if she meant the Réveil or the future Jérôme. Together they sorted newspaper clippings; as the orders arrived, looked for files on India, penicillin, or Gary Cooper, and restored order to the same jumbled files when they were returned. What irritated Lucile was the urgent, serious atmosphere of the place, and the sinister notion of efficiency that droned constantly in their ears. One week after her arrival, she had been present at a general meeting of the editorial staff, a veritable reunion of bees, buzzing with rehashed ideas—to which they had, as thoughtful tyrants, invited the ants from the ground floor and the morgue. For two hours she had witnessed, groggily, an accelerated human comedy where toadyism, conceit, gravity, mediocrity, set the pace in the general concern to augment the circulation of Jérôme's rival. Only three men had not made fatuous suggestions, the first because he systematically sulked, the second because he was managing editor and—she hoped—a nonplused managing editor, and the third because he seemed to be a little more intelligent. She had given a lively account of the meeting to Antoine, who, after having laughed warmly, had told her that she exaggerated and that she always saw the dark side of things. She had, in fact, become visibly thinner. She was so bored that she was even incapable of finishing the sandwich which—avoiding the cafeteria, having tried it for the first and the last time—she would order at noon in a nearby café, while reading a novel. At six thirty, sometimes eight o'clock—"Lucile, my dear, I'm sorry to keep you so late, but you know we're going to press the day after tomorrow"—she vainly looked for a taxi, then ended, beaten, by taking a bus, standing up usually, for she still found it repugnant to fight for a seat. She looked at the tired, worried, haggard faces of her fellow passengers, and she rebelled, more for them than for herself, because all this, for her, was but a bad dream, and she would awaken at any moment. But, at their flat, Antoine waited for her; he took her in his arms, and she knew again the feeling of being alive.

The day came when she could no longer bear it, and arriving at her café at one o'clock, she ordered a cocktail from the waiter, who was astonished, as she never drank, and then a second. She had a file to be studied, and she leafed through it for two minutes before closing it again with a yawn. Yet, they had intimated that she could write three lines on the subject, and if they were acceptable, the three lines would probably be published. But it was not possible, not today. Just as it was not possible to return to that gray office later and begin again to play her little part as the active young woman, in front of people who played the parts of thinkers or men of action. They were bad rôles, or at least it was a bad play. And if Antoine was right, if

128

this play in which she was now acting was acceptable, use-
ful, it was her part that was badly written or, in any case,
written for someone else. Antoine was wrong; she knew it
now by the violent light from these cocktails, because alcohol sometimes has pitiless, definitive spotlights and they
exposed, now, the thousands of little lies she told herself
every day to persuade herself that she was happy. A violent
self-pity invaded her. She ordered a third cocktail, and the
waiter kindly asked her what was wrong. She replied
"everything," gloomily, and he remarked that there were
days like that, that it would be better for her to order a
sandwich and, for once, to eat it, because she would end in
being tubercular like his cousin, a boy who had been in the
mountains for nearly six months. So he had noticed that
she ate nothing; so he worried about her, Lucile, who
scarcely said hello and good-bye; so somebody cared about
her. And suddenly she felt tears in her eyes. Alcohol made
her sentimental, just as it made her lucid, she had forgotten
that. She ordered the sandwich and gravely opened the
book she had borrowed from Antoine that morning. It
was *The Wild Palms,* by Faulkner, and fate led her quickly
to Harry's monologue:

"—Respectability. That was what did it. I found out
some time back that it's idleness breeds all our virtues,
our most bearable qualities—contemplation, equable-
ness, laziness, letting other people alone; good digestion
mental and physical; the wisdom to concentrate on
fleshly pleasures—eating and evacuating and fornication
and sitting in the sun—than which there is nothing better, nothing to match, nothing else in all this world but
to live for the short time you are loaned breath, to be
alive and know it— . . ."

Lucile stopped at that point, closed her book, paid the waiter, and left. She walked straight to the paper, informed Sirer that she could not continue working, asked him not to speak of it to Antoine, and gave him no other explanation. She stood before him erect, obstinate, smiling, and he looked at her, astounded. She left at once, hailed a taxi, went to a jeweler on the Place Vendôme and sold him, at half-price, the string of pearls that Charles had given her the year before as a Christmas present. She ordered a copy in imitation pearls, disdained the saleswoman's smile of complicity, and walked out into the fresh air. She spent half an hour admiring the Impressionists at the Jeu de Paume, two hours at the movies and, on reaching home, told Antoine that she was becoming accustomed to *Le Réveil*. In that way, he would not worry and she would be tranquil for a while. All things considered, she preferred lying to him to lying to herself.

She had fifteen marvelous days. Paris had returned both her idleness, and the money necessary to enjoy this idleness. She led the life that she had always led, but under false pretenses, and naturally, the feeling of playing truant enhanced her simplest pleasures. On the second floor of a Left Bank restaurant she had discovered a sort of bar-bookshop, where she passed her afternoons reading, or talking with the assembly of queer, idle, and generally alcoholic people who haunted it. One of them, a noble old man who said he was a prince, invited her, one day, to lunch with him at the Ritz and she devoted a whole hour that morning to dressing, deciding which of the little suits given her by Charles was the most fashionable. She had a fantastic, exquisite lunch at L'Espadon, with a man who gravely lied to her as he unfolded the story of his life, inspired, at the same time, by Malraux and Tolstoi, a man to whom she lied, also, in recounting to him, out of courtesy, her life by Scott Fitzgerald. So he was a Russian prince and historian; she was an American heiress rather more cultured than most. Both of them were too loved and too rich; the headwaiters fluttered about their table; they evoked Proust, whom the prince had known intimately. He paid a bill that must have permanently crippled his budget for the month ahead, and they parted, each enchanted with the other. On returning home, she recounted a thousand anecdotes to Antoine about the daily life at the Réveil; she made him laugh; she lied all the more because she loved him, all the more because she was happy and because she wanted him to share this happiness. One day, of course, he would know; one day Marianne, although she had been warned, would answer the telephone and say that Lucile had "stepped out" for a month, but, on the other hand, this menace now gave to her days an unforeseen savor. She bought ties for Antoine, art books for Antoine, records for Antoine; she talked of advances on her salary, of free-lancing, of no matter what; she was gay, and Antoine was carried away by this gaiety. With the money from the necklace she had two months clear, two months of doing nothing, of luxury and lies, two months of happiness.

Lazy, monotonous days, days all the more full for being so empty, days all the more exciting for being so peaceful, her spirit at last moving in a time without limits, without landmarks, without a goal. She recaptured the days of her youth when she systematically shirked her courses at the Sorbonne; she recaptured the sweet smell of illegality that she had lost for so long. For there was no way of measuring the leisure that Charles offered her and the leisure she stole from Antoine. And what better memory can adolescence leave behind it than that of a long and tender lie told to other people, to the future, and often to oneself? To what

131

extent did she lie to herself in running like this before what could only be a catastrophe—Antoine's anger provoked, Antoine's confidence lost, the obligation for them both to admit that she could never lead with him the normal, balanced, and relatively easy life that he proposed? She knew very well that the fact of temporarily concealing this predicament did not in the least mean that she was prepared to amend it. There was something terribly resolute in her, but for what end she did not know. In fact, she was resolved to do only that which pleased her, but that is something difficult to acknowledge when one is in love. Every night she found again Antoine's warmth, laughter, body, and not for an instant did she have the feeling that she deceived him. She could no more imagine a life without him than she could imagine a life in an office. And this alternative seemed increasingly arbitrary.

It had grown very cold and, little by little, she relapsed into her sedentary life. She got up at the same time as Antoine, went out to have coffee with him, sometimes accompanied him as far as the publishing house, returning then, officially, to her own rude labors, but in reality to their room. She undressed, went back to bed, and slept until noon. In the afternoon she read, listened to records, smoked a lot; then, at six o'clock, she remade the bed, removed the traces of her presence, and went to meet Antoine at the little bar on the Rue de Lille or, sadistically, went to the bar of the Pont Royal, where she waited until eight o'clock before regaining, seemingly exhausted, the Rue de Poitiers. There Antoine awaited her, pitied her, embraced her, and she nestled herself into this tenderness, this commiseration, this gentleness, without the least remorse. After all, she was to be pitied for having been obliged to complicate her life in this way for a man so complex. It would

have been easy to say: "I've left *Le Réveil*," and not to
have to go through her pantomime any longer. But since
this pantomime reassured Antoine, it was as well to continue. There were times when she thought herself a saint.

The day that Antoine discovered the truth, she was completely bewildered.

"I telephoned you three times this afternoon," he said.

He had thrown his raincoat onto the chair, without kiss-
ing her, and stood before her, motionless.

"I had to go out for a good two hours. Didn't Marianne
tell you?"

"Of course, of course. What time did you leave the
office?"

"About an hour ago."

"Oh?"

There was something about that "oh" that worried Lucile. She raised her eyes, but Antoine did not look at her.

"I had an appointment next door to Le Réveil," he said
rapidly. "I called you up to say I'd drop by for you. You
weren't there. So I went there directly at five thirty. That's
that."

"That's that," she repeated mechanically.

"They haven't seen you for three weeks. They haven't
given you a penny. I . . . ."

He had spoken almost in a whisper until then, but suddenly he raised his voice. He tore off his tie and threw it
at her.

"Where did this new tie come from? And these records?
Where did you have lunch?"

"Come now," said Lucile, "don't shout. . . . You don't
really believe that I've been streetwalking . . . don't be
ridiculous. . . ."

She was so surprised when Antoine slapped her that she

133

did not move for a second, even kept the little reassuring smile that she had put on. Then, she felt the warmth on her cheek and absently raised her hand to it. But this child-like gesture redoubled Antoine's fury. He had the slow, painful anger of easygoing people, more painful for the angered than for the victim.

"I don't know what you have done. I know that you have lied to me, without stopping, for three weeks. That's all I know."

There was a silence. Lucile thought of his slap; she wondered with mixed anger and amusement what would be the right thing to do. Antoine's anger always seemed to her disproportionate to the facts.

"It's Charles," said Antoine.

She looked at him, astonished.

"Charles?"

"Yes, Charles. The ties, the records, your sweaters, your life."

She understood at last. For an instant she wanted to laugh; then she saw Antoine's tormented face, his pallor, and suddenly she was dreadfully afraid of losing him.

"It's not Charles," she said very quickly. "It's Faulkner. No, listen, let me explain. The money came from the pearls. I sold them."

"You had them yesterday."

"Those are imitations, you've only to look at them. If you bit them, you . . ."

It was not the moment to advise Antoine to bite her pearls, she knew very well, or to bring up Faulkner. She was decidedly more adept with a lie than with the truth. Her cheek smarted.

"I couldn't take any more. . . ."

"After two weeks . . ."

"Yes, after two weeks. I went to Doris, the jeweler on the Place Vendôme, sold my pearls, had a copy made; that's all."

"And what did you do all day long?"

"I took walks, I stayed here, as I did before."

He stared at her, and she was tempted to look away. But it was understood, from the beginning, that in a scene of this kind to turn one's eyes away was a sign of lying. So she forced herself to stare at Antoine. His yellow eyes had darkened, and she thought vaguely that anger was becoming to him, something very unusual.

"Why should I believe you? You've lied to me continually for the last three weeks."

"Because I have nothing else to confess," she answered wearily, and she turned away. She pressed her forehead against the windowpane, absently watched a cat nonchalantly walking on the pavement, nonchalance unusual in such cold weather. She continued in a calm voice:

"I told you that I wasn't made for . . . for anything of that sort. I would die or become ugly. I was unhappy, Antoine. That's all you can blame me for."

"Why didn't you tell me?"

"You were so pleased that I should work. That I should take an interest in 'life.' I could at least pretend."

Antoine stretched out on the bed. He had spent two interminable hours of despair, of jealousy, and his rage had exhausted him. He believed her, he knew that she was telling him the truth. And this truth seemed to be appeasing and, at the same time, of a bitterness without bounds. She was alone, she would always be alone; and he wondered for an instant if he would not have preferred her to be unfaithful. He pronounced her name in a distant voice.

"Lucile . . . don't you have any trust in me?"

She was bent over him, the second after; she kissed his cheek, his brow, his eyes; she whispered that she loved him, that she loved only him, that he was crazy and stupid and cruel. He did not stop her, he even smiled faintly. He was perfectly desperate.

21

A month went by. Lucile had returned, legitimately, to her den, but now she felt a slight embarrassment when Antoine came home, to reply "nothing," always "nothing," when he asked her what she had done. In fact, he always asked the question mechanically, without acrimony, but he asked it just the same. And sometimes she saw in his eyes a look of confused sadness, of distrust. He loved her with frenzy, a deliberate fury, and afterward, as he lay on his back, when she leaned over him, it seemed that he looked at her without seeing her, that he saw in her place a boat skimming over the sea, or a cloud carried away by the wind, something moving, in any case, something that was disappearing. But he had never been more in love with her, and he told her so. Then she sank back at his side, she shut her eyes, she was silent. They say that many people forget what it means to speak, but many people forget what can be signified by being silent, the mad, fantastic, extravagant thoughts. Lucile watched, behind closed eyelids, fragments of her childhood pass by; she saw the forgotten faces of certain men, the closest, that of Charles. She suddenly recalled Antoine's tie on Diane's carpet, the shape of the big tree at the Pré-Catelan. All these memories, instead of forming the vague, homogeneous group that, when she was happy, she gaily called her life, turned into an alarming, disorderly magma now that she was less so. Antoine was right: What was to become of them? Where were they, together, heading like this? What would they become? And this bed that had been the most beautiful boat in Paris became a drifting raft, and this so familiar room an abstract setting. He had put the notion of the future into Lucile's head and, in doing so, seemed to have made it something impossible for them to share.

One morning in January, she awoke feeling violently nauseated. Antoine had already left, as he sometimes went now without waking her, as though she were a convalescent. She went into the bathroom and was sick, without being too astonished. The stockings she had been obliged to wash the evening before were drying on the little radiator, and it was in seeing them, in realizing that there were no others in her drawer, that their room was as tiny as the bathroom, in short, that she could not afford it, that she decided not to keep Antoine's child.

She had forty thousand francs remaining and she was pregnant. She was at last, after a long battle, caught and cornered by life. By what her fellow passengers on the bus submitted to as such, by what writers described as such: a world where irresponsibility was punished. Antoine loved her and would be ready to play the prospective father according to the way she presented the news. If she told him, "Something delightful has happened to us," he would take the expected child as a blessing: that she knew. But she did not have the right. Because this child would take away her freedom, and for that reason would not make her happy. And too, she knew she had disappointed Antoine and had led him to a stage in their love where everything seems to be a proof. And he would be ready to take as such this accident that was not one. She loved him too much or not enough; she did not want this baby; she wanted only him, happy, blond, yellow-eyed, free to leave her. It was doubtless her only form of honesty that, deliberately refusing any responsibility, she also refused to burden anyone else with it. This was not the time to have daydreams of a little Antoine, three years old, running about on a beach. Nor of Antoine severely correcting his son's homework. It was the time to open one's eyes, to compare the size of the room with that of a crib, a nurse's salary with that of Antoine's. It all was incompatible. There were women who could have untangled these problems, but she was not one of them. And this was not the time to daydream about herself, either.

When Antoine came home, she told him of her troubles. He grew slightly pale, then took her in his arms. He talked in a fanciful voice, and she felt herself tighten her jaws stupidly.

"Are you sure you don't want it?"

"I only want you," she said.

She did not discuss the material difficulties; she was afraid of humiliating him. And, caressing her hair, he thought that if she had wanted it he would have passionately loved a child of hers. Only, she was a runaway; that was why he loved her, and he could not reproach her for being that. He made a last effort:

"We might try to get married and all that. . . . We could move."

"Where would we go?" she asked. "And I think that a child ties one down terribly, you know. You would come home to find me fed up, in bad humor. . . . It would be . . ."

"And what, according to you, do other people do?"

"They don't do as we do," she replied, and moved away.
That was to say: "They aren't fiercely determined to be

happy." He did not answer. They went out that evening and drank heavily. The next day he asked a friend for an address.

22

The intern's face was straight and ugly, contemptuous. Lucile did not know if it was a contempt for himself or for all the women that he had relieved as best he could during the last two years, for the modest sum of eighty thousand francs. He performed the job at their homes, without anesthetics, and did not return if something went wrong. She had an appointment for the following evening, and shivered with fear and hatred at the mere idea of seeing him again. Antoine had borrowed the lacking forty thousand francs, not without difficulty, from his publisher, and, luckily, had not seen the famous intern who refused, because of a strange morality or by prudence, to meet "the guys." Otherwise, there was a Swiss doctor, near Lausanne, but that meant two hundred thousand francs, plus traveling expenses. That was out of the question, and she had not even mentioned it to Antoine. It was a smart address. No question of a private hospital, a nurse, and anesthetics for Lucile. She would give herself to that butcher of an intern, try to survive, and probably drag about for months, in poor health. It was all too stupid, too odious. And she, who had never regretted her foolishness, now thought bitterly of her pearls, sold too soon. She would end up like the heroine of *The Wild Palms*, with a fine case of septicemia, and Antoine would go to jail. She paced about in the room, like an animal; she looked at her face and slim body, pictured herself ugly, ill, whining, forever deprived of the insolently good health that played such a large part in her lust for life; she became furious. At four o'clock she telephoned Antoine; his voice sounded tired, worried, she did not have the courage to speak of her fright. Yet, at that moment, if he had asked her, she might have decided to keep the baby. But she felt him remote, helpless, and she suddenly yearned for some sort of protection. She regretted not having a woman friend with whom she could discuss such strictly feminine complications, whom she might question about these details that until now had horrified her. But she knew no woman, and her only friend had probably been Pauline. And in murmuring that name, she automatically thought of Charles. Charles, whom she had wiped out of her memory like an uncomfortable remorse, like a name that could still make Antoine suffer. In a flash, she knew that she was going to ask him for help, that no one could stop her, that he was the only human being capable of doing something to end this nightmare.

She telephoned him; she dialed the familiar office number, greeted the switchboard operator. He was there. She had a curious feeling when she heard his voice, and it took a moment for her to recover her breath.

"Charles," she said, "I should like to see you. I'm in trouble."

"I'll send the car for you in an hour," he replied calmly. "Is that all right?"

"Oh, yes, yes," she said, "in an hour."

She waited for him to hang up, and then, as he did not, she remembered his unfailing courtesy, and put down the receiver. She dressed hurriedly, and had to wait for three-quarters of an hour afterward, her brow pressed against the windowpane, for the car to arrive. The chauffeur greeted her joyfully and, with a feeling of immense relief, she sat down on the familiar seat.

Pauline opened the door and embraced her. The flat was the same as always, vast, warm, quiet, and the carpet under the English furniture was the same soft, pleasant blue. For a second, she felt badly dressed; then she began to laugh. It was something like the return of the prodigal child, but this time bringing a child of its own. The car had returned for Charles, and Lucile sat in the kitchen with Pauline and had a whisky, just as she used to do. Pauline grumbled, thought she was thinner, had lines under her eyes, and Lucile wanted to lay her head on her shoulder and allow her to settle the future. At the same time, she admired Charles's thoughtfulness in sending her alone to his house, as though it were still her house, to give her the time to become accustomed to her past, for she didn't imagine that it was, perhaps, cleverness. And when he called out from the hall, "Lucile!" almost gaily, she felt that time had gone back six months.

He too was thinner and looked older. He took her by the arm and led her into the drawing room. He firmly asked for two whiskies from a protesting Pauline, then closed the door and sat down facing her. Suddenly she felt intimidated. She glanced about the room, remarked in a loud voice that nothing had changed, and he repeated in a too tender voice that, indeed, nothing had changed, not even himself, and she thought with panic that he perhaps imagined that she had returned to him. She began to talk so fast that he had to ask her to repeat her words.

"Charles, I'm expecting a baby, I don't want to keep it, I must go to Switzerland, I have no money."

He murmured that he had imagined it would be something of the sort.

"Are you sure that you don't want to keep it?"

"I can't afford to. *We* can't afford to," she answered, blushing. "And then, I want to be free."

"You're absolutely certain that it's not only a question of money?"

"Absolutely certain," she said.

He got up, took several steps about the room; then, turning, he began to laugh sadly:

"Life is all wrong, isn't it? I would have given so much for us to have a child, and you would have had two nurses if you had wanted. . . . But you wouldn't have kept my child either, would you?"

"No."

"You don't want to have anything of your own, do you? Neither a husband nor a child nor a home . . . really nothing. It's very strange."

"I don't want to own anything," she said, "and you know that. I have a horror of possessions."

He sat down at his desk, wrote a check, and handed it to her.

"I know a very good address in Geneva. All I ask is that you go there; I shall be less worried. Will you promise?"

She nodded. She had a lump in her throat; she would have liked to cry out for him not to be so kind, so comforting, not to make her shed the tears that filled her eyes. Tears of relief, bitterness, and melancholy. She stared at the blue carpet, breathed in the odor of tobacco and leather that always pervaded the study; she could hear Pauline laughing with the chauffeur. She felt warm and sheltered.

"You know I'm still waiting for you," said Charles. "I'm horribly bored without you. It's not very tactful to tell you so today, but we see so little of each other."

He gave a small, forced laugh that put an end to her thoughts. She jumped up, muttered a hoarse "Thank you," and hurried to the door. She wept as she went down the stairs, as she had the last time, and she heard Charles call out, "Let me hear from you afterward, or get in touch with my secretary," as she walked out into the rain. She felt saved; she felt lost.

"I don't want that money," said Antoine. "Have you thought for a moment of what that man thinks of me? Does he take me for a pimp? I take his woman from him and I make him pay for my blunders?"

"Antoine . . ."

"It's too much, far too much. I'm not a model of morality, but there are limits. You refuse to have my child; you lie to me; you sell your pearls on the sly; you do no matter what just so long as it pleases you. But I won't have you borrowing money from your former lover to kill your present lover's baby. It's not possible."

"You probably think it more virtuous that I should be mangled by a butcher that *you* would pay; who would leave me to die if there were the slightest infection? You think it moral that I should be injured permanently, perhaps, so long as it isn't Charles that prevents it?"

They had turned out the red lamp and talked in whispers, sickened as they were by the horror of their discussion. For the first time, they felt a contempt for each other, and though they did not want this contempt, they could not control it.

"You're cowardly, Lucile, cowardly and selfish. At fifty, you'll find yourself alone, with nothing. Your damned charm won't work any more. You'll have no one to console you."

"You're as much of a coward as I am. You're a hypocrite. What bothers you is not that I kill the child, but that it would be Charles that paid for the operation. Your honor before my health. Where are you going to put that honor, tell me that?"

They felt cold, avoided touching each other; they felt upon them, in that large bed—which had so long been their only escape—the weight of the world. They imagined evenings alone, money worries, wrinkles, atomic missiles blasting off in a burst of fire; they saw a hostile, difficult future; they saw a life one without the other, a life without love. He knew that if he let Lucile go to Switzerland, he would never forgive himself, or her, and that it would be the end of their love. He knew that the intern was dangerous. He knew that if she kept the baby, she would be gradually exhausted by the wear and tear of time, that she would become bored, and that she would no longer love him. She was made for men, not for children; she would never be enough of an adult herself. And if one day she became adult, she would no longer like herself. All day long, he had thought: It's not possible; all women go through that one day, they have children, they have money worries, that's life, and she must understand that. She's just selfish. But when he saw her again, when he looked at her innocent, absent, unworried face, he had the impression that with her it was not a shameful weakness, but a deep, hidden, animal force that kept her from life in its most natural sense. He could not help having a vague respect for what he had despised ten minutes earlier. Untouchable. Her determination for pleasure made her untouchable, made of her selfishness what one called honesty, of her indifference, interest. He gave a peculiar moan, a moan that seemed to spring from his childhood, his birth, his whole destiny as a man.

"Lucile, I beg of you, keep the child. It's our only chance."

She did not reply. A few minutes later, he stretched out his hand toward her, touched her face. He felt the tears that fell onto her cheek and her chin; he wiped them away awkwardly.

"I'll ask for a raise," he continued; "we'll get along somehow. There are plenty of students that come to stay with children in the evening, and there is the day nursery the rest of the time . . . it's not so difficult. He will be one, two, ten years old; he will belong to us. I should have told you all this the first day. I don't know why I didn't. We must try, Lucile."

"You know very well why you didn't. You didn't believe in it. No more than I did."

She spoke calmly but she continued to cry.

"We weren't like this at first. We hid ourselves for a long time; we deceived people, we made them unhappy. We were made for lawlessness and for our own pleasure. Not to be unhappy together. We were united only for the best, Antoine, you know very well. . . . Neither you nor I has the strength to . . . do as others do."

She turned over on her stomach, laid her head on his shoulder.

"Sunshine, beaches, idleness, freedom . . . that's our due, Antoine, and we can't do anything about it. It's in our minds, under our skin. That's the way it is. We're probably what people call rotten. But I only feel rotten when I pretend to believe them."

He did not answer. He looked at the spot of light cast on the ceiling by a streetlamp; he saw again the confused expression on Lucile's face when he had tried to force her to dance at the Pré-Catelan. He recalled his own immense sadness at the sight of her tears, recalled how much he had wanted her to cry on his shoulder one night, so that he might comfort her. She was crying now and he had won, but he could not comfort her. It was not worth the trouble to lie to himself; he did not care that much about the child. All he wanted was Lucile, alone and elusive and free. Their love had always been based on anxiety, unconcern, and sensuality. He felt a great surge of tenderness; he took that half-woman, that half-child, that invalid, that irresponsible, his love, in his arms and whispered to her:

"Tomorrow morning I'll pick up the plane tickets for Geneva."

23

Five weeks passed. The operation had been brief, well done, and on her return to Paris she had telephoned Charles to reassure him. But he was not there and, with a vague feeling of disappointment, she had left a message with the switchboard operator. Antoine was occupied with a new book series that had been entrusted to him, and his situation had greatly improved, thanks to one of the numerous upheavals that had taken place in the publishing business at that time. They frequently dined with friends, associates and business connections of Antoine's, and she was surprised and delighted to see how much his personality influenced them. Lucile and Antoine never mentioned Geneva; they merely took certain precautions. This was, actually, not very difficult, as she was rather tired and he was rather worried and it sometimes happened that they simply kissed fondly before going to sleep, at first the face turned toward the other, then the back. She ran across Johnny at the Flore one very rainy afternoon in February. He was reading an art magazine, one eye cocked on a handsome blond boy seated at a nearby table; she continued on her way, but he called to her, and warmly invited her to sit down next to him at the table. He was, of course, very tanned, and he made her laugh for a long while with Claire's latest adventures at Gstaad. Diane had exchanged her Cuban diplomat for an English novelist who deceived her with young men—which obviously delighted Johnny. He absently asked for news of Antoine, and she replied in the same way. It had been a long time since she had laughed so freely, so maliciously. Antoine's friends were, as a rule, intelligent, but forbiddingly serious.

"You know that Charles is still waiting for you," said Johnny. "Claire tried to push the little de Clairvaux into his arms, but that didn't last two days. I've never seen a man yawn so much. He went from the hotel lobby to the hotel restaurant to the hotel bar, giving everybody the blues. It was frightful. What did you do to him? What do you do to men in general? I shall have need of your advice."

He smiled. He had always had affection for Lucile, and it displeased him to see her in an old suit, her hair in disorder. She still had that adolescent charm, that distant but amused expression, but she looked pale and thin. He was worried.

"You're happy?"

She answered yes, quickly, too quickly, and he guessed that she was bored. After all, Blassans-Lignières had always been charming to him; why not try to bring Lucile back to him? It would be a good deed. And he completely forgot, in the search for his motives, the violent jealousy he had felt, eight months ago, when he saw Lucile and Antoine, who were lovers of one day, gazing at each other, motionless and pale with desire, at that fashionable American's cocktail party.

"You ought to telephone Charles someday. He doesn't look well. Claire even imagines that he has some dreadful disease."

"You mean to say . . ."

"They talk so much about cancer these days. But there, I'm afraid there's some truth to it."

He lied. He was amused to see Lucile's face grow a little paler. Charles . . . Charles, so kind, so alone in his immense flat. Charles, so deserted by all the people whom he disliked, who disliked him, by all the girls flung at him for his money. Charles ill. She ought to call him up. Antoine had, as it happened, important lunch and dinner engagements for the whole of the coming week. She thanked Johnny for having told her the news, and Johnny remembered, a little late, that Claire detested Lucile. She would certainly be furious if Lucile went back to Charles. But it did not bother him to play a dirty trick on dear Claire now and then.

So Lucile telephoned Charles one morning, and they agreed to lunch together the next day. It was a fine, clear winter day, but very cold, and he found it necessary for her to have several cocktails to warm up, even as he did. The waiters' hands skimmed over the table like swallows; it was pleasantly warm, and the slight and—one could feel—futile hubbub of the restaurant made a most reassuring background. Charles ordered the menu with his usual art; he remembered all her likings. She watched him attentively, trying to detect traces of the illness in his face; actually, he looked somewhat younger than at their last encounter. She finally told him so, in a faintly reproachful voice, and he smiled.

"I've had troubles all this winter. Bronchitis that dragged on and on. But I spent three deadly weeks at a mountain resort and now it's finished."

"Johnny told me that you weren't well. . . ."

"Me? Not the least," he answered cheerfully. "You can well imagine that I would have let you know."

"Do you swear that?"

He looked sincerely surprised. "But, my God, of course I swear it. You still have a mania for putting people under oath? It's been a long time since I've had to swear to something."

He began to laugh gently, and she laughed with him.

"Johnny led me to believe that you had cancer, no less."

He stopped laughing at once.

"And that's why you telephoned me? You didn't want me to die alone?"

She shook her head:

"I wanted to see you again, too." And, to her great surprise, she realized that it was true.

"I'm alive, my dear Lucile, deplorably alive, although the dead must have more sensations than I have. I still work, and as I don't have enough courage to live alone at home, I go out." He paused, then continued in a lower voice: "Your hair is still as black, your eyes as gray. You're very beautiful."

She realized that it had been a long time since anyone had mentioned her coloring or even her physical appearance. Antoine probably thought that his lust excluded the necessity of explanations. Yet, it was very pleasant, this middle-aged man facing her, who contemplated her as an inaccessible object and not as a desire that could be gratified within the hour.

"I was wondering," said Charles, "if you would be free Thursday evening. The La Molls are having a very fine concert at their house on the Ile Saint-Louis. They're to play the Mozart concerto for flute and harp that you like so much, and Louise Vermer herself has agreed to play.

But doubtless that would be too difficult for you?"

"Why?"

"I don't know if Antoine likes music and, especially, if an invitation coming through me won't irritate him."

It was so like Charles, this invitation. He invited her with Antoine because, above all, he was polite; he preferred to see her with Antoine than not to see her at all. He would wait for her and he would get her out of all her troubles, whatever happened. And she had forgotten him for six months, and it had been necessary that she think he was at death's door for her to make herself known. How did it happen, how could he support this terrible disparity in their relations, where did he find enough substance to nourish this love, his generosity, his tenderness so poorly repaid? She leaned toward him.

"Why do you still love me? Why?"

She spoke harshly, almost grudgingly, and he hesitated for a moment.

"I could say that it's because you don't love me, which, incidentally, would be a very good reason, although incomprehensible by you, with your determination to be happy. But there's something else in you that attracted me. It is . . ." He hesitated a little, "I don't know what. An impulse, the impression of someone on the move, and Heaven knows you don't want to go anywhere. A kind of greediness, and Heaven knows you don't want to own anything. A kind of perpetual gaiety, and you rarely laugh. You know, people always look as though they were overpowered by their lives; you look as though you overpowered yours. There you are. I explain things badly. Will you have a lemon sherbet?"

"Surely it's very good for one's health," she said dreamily. "Antoine has a publishers' dinner next Thursday," she added, and it was true. "I'll come alone, if you want."

He did want it; he wanted nothing but that. They agreed to meet at eight thirty, and when he suggested "at home," she did not for an instant think of the Rue de Poitiers. The Rue de Poitiers was a room; it was not—it had never been—a home, even though it had been heaven and hell combined.

24

The La Moll house had once belonged to a state minister of some sort in the eighteenth century. The rooms were immense, the paneling superb and the candlelight, at the same time gentle and relentless (relentless because it brought out the humor—or lack of humor—of every face, gentle because it smoothed away the age), augmented the size, the charm of the drawing room. The orchestra was at the end of the room, on a kind of small stage, and, by leaning forward and avoiding the reflection of the candles in the windowpanes, Lucile could see the Seine, shining and black, twenty yards below. There was something unreal about this evening for her, so perfect were the view, the setting, the music. A year earlier she might have yawned, wished that one of the guests would slip and fall, or that a glass would break noisily, but something in her, on that evening, desperately appreciated the calm, order, and beauty that, by dint of trafficking in the colonies, the respectable La Molls afforded themselves.

"Here is your concerto," murmured Charles.

He was sitting next to her, and she could distinguish the gleam of his white shirt, his perfectly groomed hair, his long, well-kept hand holding a glass of whisky that he would offer her the moment she showed the desire. He was handsome like this, in the flickering light; he looked sure of himself and a little childlike; he looked happy. Johnny had smiled on seeing them arrive together, and she had not asked him why he had lied. The old lady bent over her harp now; she smiled faintly. The young flutist looked at her inquiringly, and one could see his throat throb. There was a very fine crowd, and it must have intimidated him. It was decidedly an evening after Proust: one was at the Verdurins', young Morel was making his debut, and Charles was the nostalgic Swann. But there was no rôle for Lucile in the magnificent comedy, any more than there had been at Le Réveil, in that frigid office three months earlier, any more than she would find one in all her life. She was neither a courtesan nor an intellectual, nor the mother of a family; she was nothing. And the first notes gently plucked from the harp by Louise Vermer brought tears to Lucile's eyes. It was music that would become increasingly tender, she knew, increasingly melancholy, increasingly irreparable, even if the last adjective could not give the idea of more or less. It was a rather inhuman music for her who had tried to be happy, to be kind, but still had made two men suffer, and who no longer knew who she was. The old lady no longer smiled, and the harp became so cruel that suddenly Lucile held out her hand to the nearest person, which was Charles, and seized his hand. That hand, that warmth, temporary surely, but living, that contact of skin, that was all that stood between herself and death, herself and solitude, herself and the fearful expectancy of that which parted or met over there, the flute and the harp, the timid young man and the old woman, suddenly equal before the blinding contempt for time of Mozart's music. Charles kept her hand in his. From time to time, with his free hand, he picked up a glass and placed it in Lucile's other hand. And she drank a lot. And there was much music. Charles's hand, long, narrow, and warm in her own, was more and more reassuring. And who was that young blond who sent her in the rain to old films, who wanted her to work, to have an abortion by a semi-butcher? Who was this Antoine who called these pleasant people rotten, the exquisite candlelight, the depth of the sofas and Mozart's music? He did not say it, of course, at least of the sofas, the candles and Mozart, but he said it of those who, at the moment, offered all that to her, plus the golden, icy, glowing liquid that ran like water down her throat. She was drunk, immobile and overwhelmingly happy, clinging to Charles's hand. She loved Charles; she loved this tender and silent man; she had always loved him; she did not wish to leave him again, and was surprised by his distressed laugh when she told him so, in the car.

"I'd give anything to believe you," he said, "but you've been drinking. It's not I whom you love."

And, of course, when she saw Antoine's hair on the pillow, his long arm stretched across her place in the bed, she knew that Charles was right. But she felt a strange regret. For the first time . . .

There were many other occasions; she still loved Antoine, doubtless, but she no longer loved loving him; she no longer cared for their life together, the lack of extravagances that a small income imposed, the monotonous days. He felt it and increased his outside activities; he almost neglected her. The empty hours that she had spent so happily in waiting had now become truly empty, because she no longer expected him as a miracle, but as a habit. She saw Charles occasionally, but she did not mention it to Antoine; it was useless to add jealousy to the resigned torment in his yellow eyes. And at night it was more a combat than an act of love to which they gave themselves. The art each had shown so long in sustaining the pleasure of the other gradually turned into a brutal technique to end things more quickly. They fell asleep reassured by their moans; they forgot that at first they had been overwhelmed.

One evening, when she had been drinking—for she drank a great deal at present—she went home with Charles. She scarcely realized what had happened. She simply thought that it was inevitable and that she must tell Antoine. She returned at dawn and woke him. Six months before, he had been in this same room, madly in love with her, whom he thought he had lost, and it was not she, but Diane who had said good-bye. He had lost Lucile for good now; he must have lacked authority or strength or something he didn't know, but he did not even try to find out what it was. For too many days he had been obstinately chewing this taste of defeat, suffering from this feeling of being powerless. He almost told her that her act was of no importance, that in any case she had always deceived him, with Charles, with life, with her own nature. But he relived that summer month, he remembered the taste of the tears she shed on his shoulder that August, and he said nothing. For over a month, since Geneva, he had expected her to leave. Perhaps, after all, there are things that cannot happen between a man and woman without permanently wounding them, no matter how free they are, and maybe the trip to Geneva was one of them. Or perhaps things had been so ordained from the start, since their fit of laughter at Claire Santré's dinner party. It would take a long time for him to recover; he realized it, looking at her drawn face, her tired gray eyes, her hand lying on the sheet. He knew every angle of that face, every curve of that body; it was geometry not easy to forget. They exchanged banal remarks. She was ashamed, she was devoid of feel-

154

ings and, doubtless, it would have been enough for him to cry out, for her to stay. But he did not make a sound.

"Anyway, you were no longer happy," he said.

"Neither were you," she replied.

They exchanged a curious, apologetic smile, distressed, but almost formal. She got up and left, and it was only when the door closed behind her that he began to sob her name: "Lucile, Lucile," and to be angry with himself. She walked back toward the flat, toward Charles, toward solitude; she knew that she was rejected forever by any life worthy of that name, and she thought that she truly deserved it.

25

They saw each other again two years later, at Claire Santré's. Lucile had finally married Charles; Antoine had been made director of a new group of publishers, and it was because of this that he had been invited. His work absorbed him and he was slightly inclined to listen to himself talk. Lucile still had charm, her happy expression, and a young Englishman called Soames smiled at her repeatedly. Antoine was seated next to her at the table; either it was chance or a last bit of malice on Claire's part, and they gravely discussed books.

"There's a French expression, *la chamade:* what does it mean exactly?" asked the young Englishman at the other end of the table.

"According to Littré, it's a roll on the drums to announce defeat," answered an erudite guest.

"How madly poetic!" cried Claire Santré, clasping her

hands. "I know that you have more words than we do, my dear Soames, but you must admit that where poetry is concerned, France reigns supreme."

Antoine and Lucile were only a yard from each other. But just as *la chamade* no longer reminded them of anything, Claire's statement no longer prompted the least bit of laughter.

N